Guns in the Heather

Guns in the Heather

Lockhart Amerman

Harcourt, Brace & World, Inc., New York

Acknowledgment

There are a number of people to whom acknowledgment for help in the background and progress of this book is gladly tendered. In addition to my secretary and the American editors, a number of Scottish friends assisted—either wittingly or otherwise. The author is particularly indebted to Dr. and Mrs. John Young of "Morlich," Midlothian. And an affectionate—and inadequate—thank-you is expressed to Agent 3.1416.

FILIO SUO

S.P.L.A.

CUIUS ACUMINE QUASI COTE

MENTEM SUAM EXACUERE SOLET

LIBRUM HUNC QUALEMCUNQUE

D.D.D.

AUCTOR

In the story that follows, no reference is intended to real persons, and any resemblance of names or titles is purely coincidental. If Dr. Fisher-Finch really exists, something ought to be done about it. As to places, some of those mentioned are real and others totally imaginary.

It was hard by the dim lake of Auber,
In the misty mid region of Weir—

—Edgar Allan Poe, "Ulalume"

Guns in the Heather

❖ 1 ❖

Just as we left the playing field, the telegram was handed me by one of the modern-language masters. Clammy Krohten, we called him. "Clammy" was a nickname, of course, but it suited him right down to the ground. Unfortunately, he was a refugee from somewhere, so you were supposed to make allowances. And I don't doubt that he knew his German and Russian. The fact remained that he was utterly unlovely and a kind of academic creep.

As I say, he handed me the telegram—just as we all were leaving the Old Field. Being reasonably sure of what was in it, I stuffed it into my pocket and kept on going. Confirmation of arrangements from my father, I thought. He was to pick me up at the school in the early evening, and together we would start for a holiday up north. I hadn't seen the Boss since the previous autumn, and nine months in a British boarding school is a long time.

My bath over, I found Tommy Grant waiting for me in my room. Tommy is a fat, jolly sort of character who likes to talk jive with a Glasgow accent.

"Good throw, daddy-o!"

"Thanks, Tommy," I said. "Pure baseball, I'm afraid."

It *had* been a pretty good heave at that—two-fifty, at least. And I'd been lucky enough to smash the runner's wicket—rather like getting someone at the plate with a peg from the outfield. All very productive of a satisfied feeling in the midriff, especially when the runner had represented their last out. The "foolish Fettesians" were going home with a crimp in their record. The last day of school and—

"Where's the ruddy hero?" It was Alec Macnicol's voice in the doorway. (Alec is really the Master of Inchdarroch and an Honorable. For someone whose father is a lord, he's surprisingly normal.)

"Deft," said Alec, "very deft. He fired the shot heard round the world. Good old Posy, the boy who brought the Polo Grounds to Scotland!"

"The Polo Grounds," I told him, "almost went west with the Giants. What you people don't know about baseball would fill a bookcase."

Tommy disagreed. "We dig it, mon, but good."

"Help the lad on with his flannels," said Alec. "You know—a hero even to his valet."

They started to insert me forcibly into my trousers when I remembered the telegram. Alec fished it gingerly from the pocket of my cricket clothes and held it out to me.

"What's this? Fan mail so quickly?"

I started to uncrumple it. "Just a wire from the Boss. He's picking me up, you know."

So I thought till the paper lay unfolded in my hand.

"My word!" I said mildly, though a queer sort of apprehension grabbed at my voice. The telegram read:

UNAVOIDABLY DELAYED MR FINCH WILL MEET YOU WAVERLEY STEPS 2015 TODAY WEAR BLAZER BRING GEAR HASTA LUEGO BOSS

The others listened as, de-trousered, I went over it aloud.

"Sounds mysterious," said Tommy, forgetting his favorite jargon for a moment.

"Not so mysterious if you know my father," I answered. "But I certainly thought he'd come himself. His last letter was quite definite."

"Who's this Finch individual?" Alec wanted to know.

"Never heard of him. Some pal of Father's, I suppose. But how am I going to know him? There may be hundreds of Finches hopping about on Waverley Steps." (But I could hear my father's voice: "If ever I have to send someone to fetch you, Jonny, you'll know by this grip that he's real." And I could feel the Boss's fingers grasping mine in a special pattern.)

"Vice versa," Tommy said. "He's to know you. Wherefore the blazer."

Alec agreed. "Quite. Quite. You are the gent with the lilac nosegay, carrying a folded newspaper and managing to look inconspicuous. Really, I love this. Will Finch, by any chance, be your father in disguise?"

It was an intriguing idea, but despite some experience of the Boss's whimsies, I didn't think he'd be passing himself off as someone else. At any rate, not to me.

"Come on, you guys, help me pack." (British boys, I have found, like to be called "guys" by an American. It makes them feel that they're part of a gangster movie or something.) "The wire said, 'Bring gear.' I wonder which? The Boss and I were going to do some climbing—"

"Finch doesn't sound like a mountain man to me," Alec said. "Here—shirts—and of a dainty hue—socks ditto—spare tie, red and white of course—what Forsyth's call 'body linen'—"

"I can send back for the boots, I suppose—when I know where we're going."

"Certainly you can; old MacDuff will be happy to hear from you." (MacDuff is the school porter.) "And by the by"—Alec was tugging at a pack strap—"don't forget *my* invitation. The family'll be at Inchdarroch till the middle of the month, and nothing would please them more, et cetera. Master Grant's coming up; aren't you, Thomas?"

"Like I dig ye, mon," said Tommy. Then he asked me a question. "What's with this 'loogo' talk—in yon telegram?"

"Oh," I told him, "that's Spanish. It simply means 'so long.' But it's a kind of code, too. Whenever the Boss breaks into Spanish, it means the message is important and I've got to do exactly what he says."

"Like meeting Finches?"

"Like meeting Finches."

"Curiouser and curiouser," commented the Master of Inchdarroch. "I've a notion, Posy, that you're headed for adventure."

He hadn't the slightest idea how right he was. Nor had I, as the bus bore me swiftly past the lights of Portobello and up the crowded bustle of Leith Walk.

2

At this point perhaps I'd better introduce myself. My name is Jonathan Flower (hence "Posy"), and I live in a place called Wynnewood, which is a suburb of Philadelphia. That is, I live there when I'm not at school in Scotland or trying to catch up with the Boss on one of his expeditions. Ever since World War II, the Boss has had a job with the government. It is very hush-hush and has taken him literally to the ends of the earth. The den at Wynnewood is lined with everything from kukri knives to blowpipes. I once read about the Boss that he is a "master of weaponry"—and I guess he is.

I have been a problem for him ever since my mother died and left him to look after a three-year-old baby. He's done his best. For the last few years we've had long vacations together; he's taken me shooting and climbing and helped me with languages and some of the many odd knowledges he has; and once in a while he's told me strange tales of strange people. But I've learned that his business is his own and most of it a secret. In consequence, he's had to park me, much of the time, in schools here and there, and there have been stretches when I haven't seen him—or even heard from him except for an occasional letter—for months on end. Which may, I suppose, explain why we get along better than a good many fathers and sons.

As I've said, my latest stopping place had been a Scottish school just outside Edinburgh, where—quite apart from lessons—they taught me a number of things. One was not to underestimate either a big-school accent or a broad Scots burr. Another was to get a kick (forgive the expression!) out of rugby. And although I know that it sounds un-American, I became purely fascinated by cricket. With the exception of Mr. Krohten aforesaid, I liked the masters. As for the holidays, I was very lucky about invitations —to Wales for Christmas and to Speyside for Easter, plus a couple of weekends with Tommy Grant's people near Paisley.

All year sporadic letters reached me from the Boss, first from Hong Kong, then from the States, most recently from Switzerland. It was this last one that had told me of his plan to come to Scotland in time for the end of term. Then—the telegram . . .

The bus swung into Princes Street and pulled up at the traffic island opposite the North British Hotel. Gripping my pack, a fairly small one, I made for the head of the stairs. The tower clock said eight-five (or 2005 in my father's idiom) and shrugging off the raincoat I had worn over my blazer, I stationed myself against the low wall above the Gardens.

It was full daylight, of course; the pavements were crowded with strollers, talkers, sweethearts, and movie-goers. Everything was busy and matter of fact. Yet for some reason—or for lack of it—I felt a creeping chill. Ordinarily, I was able to take the Boss's unpredictability for granted. But now I began to wonder about his change of plans, the telegram. I wondered whether he had actually sent it.

A hoarse voice broke in on my musing.

"Well, well, if it isn't the Posy, decked for summer!"

"Hello, Flower. Well thrown today—very."

"Waiting for someone, my boy?"

Three sixth-formers from the school had come up the stairs from the station behind me. I felt a little embarrassed by the blazer: our colors are not inconspicuous.

"How about a lobster at the Café Royal?"

"We've hours to kill before the Night Scotsman."

They jabbered of the joys of London, where, it was obvious, several nightclubs yearned for their patronage. Then they strolled away with "Cheers!" and "Good summer!" and I was left at my post.

The clock said eight-fourteen. Three women hurried past and down the steps, intent on a suburban train. A squadron of traffic halted for the light, then ground away in a spasm of gears.

I had turned to look the length of the Gardens when a soft voice spoke directly in my ear.

"Mr. Jonathan Flower, I think?"

He was a short, wide man, several inches smaller than I am but giving the impression of vast strength. Although the evening was warm, he wore a topcoat of dark material buttoned well up to his chin. Under the brim of his bowler, I noticed that his left eye was fixed and crooked. How he had crept up on me so silently I had no idea, though I was to learn later that lightness of foot was one of his many unusual gifts.

"Mr. Finch?"

He nodded. "You will come with me."

"Yes, sir. My things are here." I pointed to the knapsack. "Has my father—"

"Not now," said Mr. Finch. "There is no time. A little later." He looked warily over his shoulder, as if he were afraid of being seen in my company. "See—we are attended."

A black taxi had pulled up at the curb, and my new friend turned and started for it. There was nothing to do but follow. Mr. Finch held the door, and I read the driver's name, G. L. Gillan, neatly printed on it in the ordinary way of Edinburgh cabs. I took the far seat, and no sooner was my guide beside me than we were off with a lurch. The meter read "10/6," and I concluded that Mr. Finch had already enjoyed quite a journey. He gave the driver no directions.

"My father—" I said. "Do you have any definite information about him?"

The cab swung left on Lothian Road and kept straight on. I didn't know this part of the city very well, and I was lost in no time. The driver began to weave, turning at nearly every corner, till I gave up trying to read street signs. Gradually the traffic fell away, but Mr. Finch made no answer to my question.

Instead, he suddenly said, "I must trouble you to put this on."

I thought at first it was a scarf that he held in his hand —dark cloth it was—but with a gesture of surprising swiftness he slipped the thing over my head, and I was blindfolded—hooded like a hawk.

I started to shout a protest and snatched at the mask, or

whatever it was, when fingers like steel bit into the muscle between my neck and my shoulder. It didn't hurt me very much, but it paralyzed me absolutely.

"One regrets," said Mr. Finch, "but it is necessary. Consider please the safety of your father and make no difficulty." The pincers relaxed a little. "You will wish to do as your father has ordered. It is only for a few moments. Assure me please that you will not disturb the bandage." He spoke with no discernible accent but in a stilted way— as if he were talking a translation. As for doing what he asked, apparently I had small choice.

"All right," I told him gruffly. "If my father really ordered this—this—"

"It is his wish." And Mr. Finch was silent.

All this time the taxi had been scooting along at a good clip, slowing a little to corner, then speeding on. We had left all trace of cobbles and were moving on the smooth surface of a major road.

Perhaps I should have made a struggle then and there. At one point I nearly threw caution away and had tensed myself to tear at the blindfold; but he seemed to read my mind.

"Remember please. It is but for a little time more."

I relaxed a bit, but I had the feeling in my darkness that he watched me.

We were on cobblestones again when the cab pulled to a stop. Mr. Finch made no motion to pay, and apparently the driver was used to blindfolded passengers, for he made no remark as I was bustled, rather than aided, onto the sidewalk.

"My pack—" I said.

"I have it here," said Mr. Finch. I heard the sound of a gate click open and snap behind us. "This way. Two steps now. Soon—in a minute—you will see again."

The man's manner was not unkind, and my misgivings lessened. Another step—this time through a door, for my foot caught on the sill. Then across carpet, up a stairway—one flight, then another, forty-four steps in all—and a door closed behind us.

"Now we may remove the apparatus," Mr. Finch announced. Quick, strong fingers twisted at the blindfold. Then it was gone.

A bright light shone at me from a table lamp, and for a little space I could see nothing else. Then I made out the figure of my companion standing in the shadow at the far side of a desk.

"For the present," he said, "you will remain here."

I had had just about enough. "I don't understand at all," I said. "I know my father has to do things in an odd way sometimes, but this business certainly calls for some sort of explanation. Where am I? And where is my father? And why this nonsense with the blindfold?"

Pertinent questions they seemed to me, but they made small impression. Mr. Finch looked me over in exasperating silence, then resumed his former theme.

"For the present you will remain here. This is a safe house," he added. "Do you know what that means?"

A safe house? It meant what it sounded like, didn't it? Then I remembered that my father had used the phrase now and then in a technical sense. American agents operating on foreign soil, he had explained to me, sometimes established secret headquarters—in a shop, a private house, in every kind of place provided it had the appearance of ordinary innocence. Known only to the agent's closest colleagues, these "safe" houses were used for refuge, rest, and, I guessed, rearmament. The man called Finch was telling me that I had been brought to such a place. Even in placid Edinburgh, it seemed, there was a need for secret hideaways.

"So." It was as if he followed my thoughts. "I see that you understand." And with that he turned and left the room.

My eyes had now grown used to the light, and I examined my new surroundings. It was an old house, I gathered—not old as Edinburgh houses go, but no new villa in the suburbs. Walnut woodwork framed the high bay window, and the general gloom was deepened by brown paper covering the inside of the panes. A second door gave on a shallow closet, empty save for some weary dustcloths drooping from a hook. A chest of drawers topped with bookshelves stood against the wall. In the center of the room was the lamplit desk. A couch and two or three chairs completed the furnishing.

I walked to the door by which I had entered and found that it opened on a short, dark hall. To the left was a bathroom. Beyond the bathroom, another door. I tried it. It was locked.

I decided to investigate the windows and found that they, too, were locked or spiked in some manner—apparently from the outside. Using my pocketknife cautiously, I cut a slit in the brown paper, but nothing could be seen: storm shutters of very solid wood had been closed over the windowpanes. Was I, I asked myself, a protégé or a prisoner? The alliteration rather pleased me.

A search of the room seemed to be indicated. Any clues

to my whereabouts would be welcome—but there was nothing very helpful. The single drawer of the desk contained a dried-up inkwell, a pencil stub, and a post card mailed from Copenhagen to "J. van Hoost, Caledonian Hotel, Edinburgh" with the singular message: "Pastry prices off, poor market for éclairs, iced buns continuing as per order." There was an indecipherable scrawl for a signature, but the subject matter made me realize I was hungry.

Whereupon, someone knocked at the outer door in the hallway.

"It's locked," I said. "I can't open it."

A woman's voice answered me. "Ech no, it winna be locked. Come on then. I've both hands full of tea."

I went to the door, and sure enough, it opened readily, admitting a very welcome sight. I refer both to the lady and her burden. She was medium in age and height, with a high color in her pleasant face and big bright eyes. In both hands, as advertised, she held a tray of tea things. I took it from her with more speed than chivalry.

"Ye'll be starving, poor fellow," she said comfortably. Her voice and her person both reminded me of the good Scots adjective "soncy."

"Have ye things?" she asked. "You're to bide the night, ye know."

I didn't know, and I stopped pouring tea to tell her. "Thanks very much for the tea," I said, "but I don't know about anything. Can you tell me where I am?"

She laughed at that. "At the doctor's, of course," she said. "We've not had a resident patient this long while."

"The doctor's? What doctor's?"

"Come away with ye," she said. "Dr. Fisher's, to be sure

22

—as if ye were that daft. The doctor'll be up, whiles, to see that you're snug—so take your bit tea now; there's a good lad." The conversation struck her as very amusing, for she burst into another peal of laughter.

"Look here—" I hesitated.

"The name's McGregor," she told me, "Mrs. Mc-Gregor."

"Yes. Thank you. But Mrs. McGregor, I don't know any Dr. Fisher. I'm not a patient. I came here because my father—" But I couldn't go into a long explanation with her, and besides, I was beginnng to feel panicky. "It's very complicated," I said. "I'd like to see Mr. Finch. I can't explain. Could I possibly see Mr. Finch?"

She gurgled again with sheer happiness. "There's nae finch in *this* roost. Get on with ye, laddie. Eat your tea. There's a bit sandwich forby—under yon cover."

So there was. And for the moment I gave up the argument and sank my teeth into ham-on-toast. The meat was tender and the tea was strong. I wondered whether all "safe" houses were manned by madcaps.

Mrs. McGregor decided to take herself off. "I'll be back in a wee while for the tray."

I left my repast long enough to try the door after her. It was locked again.

❖ 3 ❖

But Mrs. McGregor was not my next caller. I was drinking the last of the tea when—without warning—the door opened, and the man Finch walked into the room. The bowler was gone, and he had changed his dark coat for a white one; but in spite of the fact that I had never had a really good look at him, I recognized the strong, squat figure and the wonky eye. A strap around his head held one of those lights that doctors look down people's throats with. He even had a small black bag in his hand.

"Good evening, my boy," he said, and I nearly jumped out of my skin, for though the man was undoubtedly the same, his voice was altogether different. The clipped staccato of his former speech had suggested somehow that his English was acquired. Now he spoke in smooth professional accents.

"I'm glad you've had your tea. Bit of a bracer after a long day, eh?"

I didn't think it necessary to inform him that I'd tucked in pretty well at school. Instead, I headed for what seemed to me the heart of the matter.

"Mr. Finch," I began—but he raised a finger in correction.

"Fisher," he said, "Dr. Fisher."

Could I possibly have misheard him at Waverley Steps, I asked myself? Then I remembered that he had never actually announced his name. But the Boss's telegram had spelled it out—F-I-N-C-H.

"Mr. Finch, Dr. Fisher—whatever your name is—will you please explain what's up? I'm utterly confused. Did my father send you to meet me or not?"

Instead of answering, he looked at me the way a botanist would look at an unfamiliar aphid. Then he spoke, but it was half to himself.

"Your father? Ah, yes. Poor boy—he's forgotten. You have no father, Donald."

Partly I was afraid, but mostly—angry.

"My name's not Donald, and I most certainly have a father," I told him. Out of the corner of my eye I saw that he was fumbling with the clasps of his little black bag.

"Poor boy," he said.

"Poor boy, my foot!"

I started to push past him for the door, but with unexpected speed he caught me by the wrist, thrust out his knee, and spun me round in such a way that I stood with my back to him. Instantly I felt the pincer grip between my neck and shoulders, harder this time than before.

I was powerless as a paralytic in his grasp. And then out of the corner of my eye I caught the gleam of chrome, and a hot needle-thrust of pain pierced my upper arm.

He gave me a push and stood away from me, breathing a little fast.

"You must be quiet, Donald." His voice was still professional. "You will be quiet, will you not? I have given

25

you something to ease your nerves." He glanced at the hypodermic gleaming in his hand.

As for me, my shoulder felt as if it had been severed from my body, and a weakness like nausea welled up from the pit of my stomach. I'm not a bad boxer, if I do say so, and I used to wrestle a bit at school in the States; but right then I had no backbone for this Fisher-Finch and his tricky tactics. What I did, I'm afraid, was simply to sulk.

"Sit on the sofa there," he told me. "Here, I'll have your blazer. That's it; loosen the tie. That's it. And listen to me. We've got a minute or two left for talk. . . . Listen to me.

"Your name is Donald Buckman. You know that, don't you? You are an orphan boy from Canada, and you answered my advertisement. You telephoned, didn't you? And you agreed that as my junior assistant, you would subject yourself to certain tests, didn't you?"

I let myself lean drowsily back on the couch.

"The tests have started, haven't they, Donald? You're a willing assistant now, aren't you? So. Good enough." He looked at me for a long silence, then packed and closed his bag. "Good night, Donald." He switched out the lamp on the desk, and I heard him cross the room and close the outer door behind him.

For a few minutes I fought whatever it was that he had given me, but the stuff was strong. I made a brief and futile attempt to remove my clothing but settled for kicking my shoes off.

Still struggling against the dope, I felt myself drifting off into sleep. From somewhere, a thought was trying to get through to me: I had forgotten something—something I had promised myself to do, something that was important. . . . Oh yes, I knew: I had never tested Fisher-Finch with the Boss's handclasp. At Waverley Steps I had forgotten all about it. After that, there had been no opportunity. . . .

When I woke, the shining figures on my wrist watch indicated half-past four. From the darkness of the room I had no way of telling whether it was day or night, and for a moment or two I lay still, recollecting myself and waiting for a headache that did not materialize. Whatever the doctor had given me must have been remarkably nutritious. I wondered what had waked me.

Then I heard it. It was a scraping sound, not loud but, in the silence of the room, distinct. It stopped. Then, as I sat up, it began again, originating as I thought in the direction of my feet beyond the end of the sofa.

Again a scratching, and I thought of rats. Nothing more likely in an old house, I told myself. I swung my feet over the side and felt warily for my shoes. In the pitchy darkness of the room, the desk was hard to find, but as I stood with my hand on the lamp switch, I heard the noise again —across from me—in the wall, perhaps.

I turned the switch, and nothing happened. Even an extra flick or two—in case the lamp were one of those multiple gadgets—made no difference. Everything stayed black, not with the mixed intensity of ordinary darkness but with an unrelieved, impenetrable gloom.

I stumbled back to the sofa, felt for my blazer, and remembered that the doctor had hung it neatly on the back of a chair. My hands encountered it, felt for the inner pocket, and drew out the shape of a fountain pen. My belongings, apparently, had not been disturbed.

With a prayer for the battery, I pressed a tiny button,

and the pocket flashlight shot out a slim white beam. On the wall from which I thought the sound had come, it made a small bright circle and hovered to a stop on the door of the empty closet. The cracks and wrinkles of the ancient wood were visible, and the black porcelain of the doorknob gave back a dull reflection. I shifted the light down toward the wainscoting, half expecting to encounter beady eyes or a scurrying shape.

But something white lay on the floor, half protruding from the inside of the closet. My small light showed a scrap of paper. I snatched it up, and it rustled—exactly like my fancied rat.

Under the close-held beam, there was a scrawl of penciled writing, faint and wobbly and hard to read. For what good it did me, I made it out: "Milkman stops at six—don't forget." That was it. Nothing else.

Of all the senseless, useless finds! A note for Mrs. McGregor, no doubt—a routine household reminder. And then I caught my breath, for I *knew,* I was absolutely certain, that the note had not been on the floor or in the closet when I searched the room before tea. Somehow—from somewhere—it had arrived since my session with the doctor!

Indeed, as I thought of the scratching sound that had awakened me, I was sure that I had actually heard the paper moving into place. My mind went back to a thrilling book by Michael Innes in which educated rats were used to carry messages—but not to place them neatly under door cracks!

I opened the closet and shone my pencil beam around the dark interior. The dustcloths still hung dankly from their hook, and a musty odor of disuse prevailed. Carefully, I examined the interior, sides and back, but there was nothing to be seen like a slit or a hinge. The message about the milkman had walked into place by itself!

Still clutching the scrap of paper, I turned off my light to conserve the battery and was about to give the whole thing up as the aftereffects of Dr. Fisher-Finch's medicine when, in the pitchy black, my eye was caught by the faintest of glows at the back of the closet. It was a hairline difference in the darkness, nothing more—but the difference was there!

Foolishly, I snapped my light on and saw nothing. I cut it off and closed my eyes, deliberately counting to thirty to reaccustom them to darkness. I looked again, and the thread-thin vertical of white was there!

It had to be a crack.

I clipped the torch into the pocket of my shirt and felt the rear wall with my fingers. The crack was there, for I could blot out its tiny light with my hand; but so minute was it—or so carefully carpentered—that it made no more impression on my touch than the ordinary grain of the wood. And as I probed and patted, suddenly the vein of light was gone—not dimming slowly or fading away, but all at once, as if a lamp, wherever it was behind the wall, had been turned out.

I kept my hand in place and waited. If the silly dairy message had arrived this way, there had to be an opening. And if lights in the next room were turning on and off, there had to be someone there to turn them. And the chances were that somebody had used the opening to thrust a foolish message about milk into my room.

I made up my mind. Digging my thumbnail noiselessly into the wood as nearly as I could to where the crack had shone, I left a small but palpable cut in the wall. With the help of my flashlight, I crossed to the door of the room and tried it. As I expected, it was locked. From my pack on the floor, I removed an elderly green pullover; the room was cold, and I put the sweater on. Into my pocket went a small Quintax A260 camera, together with my toothbrush and a comb. Investigation showed that my modest store of cash was unimpaired. I closed the pack and put it back exactly where it had been. Laying my folded raincoat on the floor within easy reach, I set to work once again on the back of the closet. My watch said five-fifteen. If I should find an opening, I was ready to go wherever it led me.

❖ 4 ❖

In the beginning, my thumbnail slit eluded me, but after a bit of reconnaissance by fingertip, I found the tiny blaze. The crack itself was invisible, and with no hairline light to guide me, I fumbled uselessly against the unrevealing wood. The slimmest blade of my knife occurred to me as a useful probe, but for what seemed like ages, I encountered only solid oak.

I had almost given up when, instead of stubbing itself on sheer wall, the paper-thin steel thrust easily away from me to the depth of at least an inch. Working as I was, devoid of sight, I found that my other senses seemed to have acquired an extraordinary keenness. Very gently I moved the knife blade upward. It caught for a moment, then slid freely for a foot or so before it stuck again.

I tried a downward motion, and the results were still better. Apparently, I could run my slender probe all the way to the floor.

I knelt to prove it and had come within six inches of the bottom when my knife gave a little tug—like the first faint nibble on monofilament. There was an almost inaudible click. The back of the closet moved silently aside, and I was looking from the darkness of my own into the shadows of another room.

The bulk of an upholstered chair loomed straight before me, and I guessed that it was purposefully placed to block the secret entrance. On hands and knees, like a child playing lion, I peeked around the obstacle—and saw nothing but the shapes of other furniture all vaguely blue in the half-light that leaked from a heavily curtained window. Reaching back, I picked up my mackintosh, shrugged into it, and closed the closet door behind me. With some idea of covering my tracks, I tried to coax the sliding panel back in place, but it would not budge. I decided to waste no more time on it.

The room was carpeted and quite tenantless. Whoever had been turning lights off and on—and possibly shoving the morning mail under door cracks—had departed. Whereas my prison chamber had been brown and bleak, this room was handsomely painted in a pale shade against which moldings and borders were etched in gold. A pendant crystal chandelier added to the festive eighteenth-century décor. Mentally, I saluted the decorators and looked for the nearest exit.

It gave on a hall, which I entered almost directly at the head of the stairway—the same stairway, I was certain, up which I had been led the night before. Twenty-two steps per flight, as I remembered, and I peered down into the murky well, darker as it receded from the oval skylight high above.

If you have ever had occasion to prowl through a perfectly strange house in the early morning—without the slightest knowledge of either its geography or its inhabitants—you have some notion of my sentiments. I had no wish to get lost, and even less to encounter the amiable doctor.

As I stood and pondered the prospect, a door opened on the floor below me. Light spilled out dully from a room at the back, and I heard voices talking. I was unable to distinguish any words, but the rhythm didn't sound like English. As long as the conversationalists remained where they were, I could take a chance on slipping by them to the lower flight. This gained, I stopped and listened out of sheerest curiosity. They were speaking what I recognized to be Chinese!

Aside from a few stock phrases gathered from my father, I know as much of the celestial dialects as I do of Middle Amharic. Nor could I readily imagine a less likely place or time for oriental chit-chat than an Edinburgh suburb in the early-pearly morning. I was just about to continue my downward way when one of the talkers said something *un*-Chinese and vaguely reminiscent. It was a name. Not a British or an American name, but a name I knew. It was the name of "Jan van Hoost." I had a post card addressed to the gentleman in my pocket.

I reached the street floor and headed around the black wrought-iron stair rail to the after-quarters. The gaining daylight twinkled on a silver tea set as I passed the dining room. At the back of the corridor, I pushed aside a swinging door of baize and found myself in a kitchen gleaming with the white and chrome of domestic catalogues. "Lucky Mrs. McGregor," I thought, wishing I knew where she stored yesterday's bannocks.

Somewhere in the house a clock struck six. As the last note died away, I heard from the direction of the street the soft clop-clopping of a rubber-shod horse. This part of the city, it seemed, still got its milk by the older fashion of delivery.

Over a brick wall at the end of the kitchen garden, I saw the top of a white-painted wagon slow and stop. As I drew back from the window, a gate in the wall swung open, and a man in white cap and duster came up the garden path. He was of slight build and less than medium height; the upturned colar of his duster hid his face except for a blond mustache. At the doorstep he deposited a rack of white bottles. His back was toward me as he straightened up and stretched his arms out horizontally. At a casual glance he appeared to be welcoming the morning with a gigantic yawn. But his hands were moving in a queer gesture, rotating at the wrists. It was the "come on" motion of a traffic policeman. Suddenly things began to fall into place.

The note beneath the door had been intended for me. Had anyone else found it, it would have passed for an ordinary household memorandum. The only hitch—and it might have been a fatal one—was that I was given credit for more brains than I had. The idea of mere coincidence ought never to have entered my head.

Thinking these thoughts, I let myself out of the kitchen door. A chain latch hung across it, and I gave a brief look for alarm connections—but nothing happened; no bells or sirens sounded, and I stepped onto the garden path just as the milkman disappeared through the gate.

Sprinting a little, I was on his heels as he climbed into the wagon.

He picked up the reins and said, "Come along then." It wasn't clear whether he was speaking to me or the horse, but I took the words for invitation as the vehicle began to move and hopped up beside him through the opening amidships. The rig was one of those well-ventilated models where the driver stands and passengers are not expected. The interior smelled not unpleasantly of cheese.

To right and left, a neighborhood of free-standing houses with walled gardens and high gates spoke of peace and a measure of prosperity. The morning sky was a misty blue, and though the confines of the wagon hindered sight of the horizon, I had an idea we were south of the southeast suburbs. Our horse ambled onward, and I glimpsed a street sign: "Forfar Loan." Beneath it an arrow pointed to "Glenlivet C. C.—Grounds."

I felt a movement beside me. The driver was turning down the collar of his duster. Next he took off his cap and whipped the mustache from his upper lip.

I have said that I had not had a decent look at him, though of course I had wondered what manner of milkman made a habit of rescuing schoolboys imprisoned on his route. Now I knew: to my utter delight and astonishment, the milkman was my father!

❖ 5 ❖

"Take the reins a minute, will you, Jonathan?" Such was his greeting as he turned to rummage in the rear of the wagon. "Hector certainly gives an impression of mildness, but they tell me there is fire in his soul."

Hector, I took it, was the horse. Aside from this realization, I was stupefied.

"Glad we got you out of the dungeon all right. I wasn't sure about communications. Here, put this on." He handed me the duster. "Whoa, Hector. We'll just stop here for a minute."

With his hand over mine, he guided our steed to the curb and a halt. The street was trafficless and very quiet.

"I have to talk pretty quickly, I'm afraid." He was pulling on a grubby-looking jacket over his turtleneck jersey. "I only missed you at school by ten minutes, you know."

"You—you missed me at school?"

"Sure. Arrived in my own person, I'm glad to say. Tall boy—what's his name?—Macnicol, that's it. Macnicol told me about the telegram. Found it for me in your wastebasket. I never sent it, of course."

"But the 'hasta luego'—" I protested. (The Spanish tag had swept away any thought of suspicion.)

"Very clever of them, that part. So was using Finch's name. You remembered it, I suppose?"

Dimly, it seemed to me, the name in the telegram had not been wholly unfamiliar. At the time I hadn't really stopped to think; now I knew that "Finch" should have meant something.

"He was the bird you met last summer at Bar Harbor —a participant, shall we say, in the business of Senator Thatch—"

I remembered now. But I had scarcely more than seen the man.

"Good technique," my father went on. "Playing on the transient recollection. As for the Spanish, someone in the opposition knows us pretty well."

"But what about this Dr. Fisher? And the house I was in? How did you—"

"Take it easy. There isn't time right now for a real explanation. I might say that after I talked with your schoolmate, I beat your bus to Waverley Steps. Afraid I left the school in a tearing hurry and probably made the boys wonder."

"You were at Waverley Steps before I was?"

"Absolutely. Saw you arrive, admired your gaudy garment, and watched you watch the clock. Didn't you notice the old bird with the spiked stick, picking up scraps of paper that weren't there?" I shook my head. "Well, that was me. I saw your friend in the derby arrive but didn't manage to overhear the conversation. I was just making up my mind to introduce myself when he whisked you off to that phony taxi. I couldn't very well climb on the fender: there was a cop coming closer every minute. So I noted the cab-number, quit my rag-picking, and scooted along Princes Street in your wake. You had too good a start."

"But how did you find the house?"

"That'll have to wait. It's time now to give you some instructions. I have an appointment."

"You mean we can't—"

"Stick together? Not right now. If everything goes well, I may see you tonight. In the meantime, hear this. Listen very carefully. For the moment, you're safe. But you're only safe as long as they don't know where you are. The minute you're spotted, you'll be followed; and very soon after you're followed, you'll be nabbed; and the minute you're nabbed, I'm in the soup.

"Somehow or other, you see, they found out about your being at school and my plan to pick you up. As it happens, I'm rather in their hair right now, and by holding you, they think they've got me stymied. But as long as I know you're safe, I'm free to act. Therefore—"

I couldn't help interrupting. "Father, you mustn't worry about me. You've always said that in the service nothing interferes—"

"Don't be silly, Jonathan. People in the service are human, whatever it says in the storybooks. Your job right now is to do as I tell you—and this is it: Take this milk wagon as far as you can. Keep straight ahead, and in just about a mile you'll come to Clark Street. Turn right and carry on into Nicolson. You'll see a pub on your right called the 'Faithful Friend.' I can't promise you, but there ought to be a chap there to relieve you. In any case, ditch the rig and get on into the city. You've got to get in to get out, I'm afraid."

A new MG pulled into the street ahead of us, and he

ducked into the back part of the wagon. The car passed us, apparently without notice.

"Now here's the rest of it. Stay away from the Bridges and Princes Street—at least as long as you can. They'll expect you to head for *people*—the busy streets where it's easy to lose a tail. So we'll cross 'em up and stick to the byways. You'd better go west through Chambers Street; then skirt the Castle till you come out on Lothian Road. Take a Number 144 bus from in front of the 'Cally' and stick with it till you're out in the country past Kirknewton. A mile farther, and you'll see an Esso station. Get off there and take the dirt road right—to Plummet Lodge. They'll be expecting you—I hope. *Compris?*"

"I think so. Bus 144 past Kirknewton. An Esso station. Right to Plummet Lodge. What's Plummet Lodge?"

"It's a farm. Kind of a fancy one. When you reach it, ask for Sophia."

"Sophia? A woman?"

"Yes. One of those. Have any money? Here." He handed me three pounds, brand new. "Once you're at the lodge, wait till I call."

You never see my father really fussed, but I sensed a certain tension in him. Obviously, he wanted to get the show on the road. I ventured a final question.

"You think I'll be followed?"

"I don't have any idea. With luck, no. But I'll bet they're thinking hard. There's probably a squad of them on Princes Street right now. So—I'll leave you." Without the slightest affectation, he held out his hand. I clasped it, felt the signal grip; and he dropped from the step of the wagon. I barely heard his soft "Good Luck!" and I watched him through the small rear window as he walked back to the crossing, a rather disreputable figure, making remarkable time for a man with a limp. At the corner, he disappeared.

"Gitty-up, Hector," I said, flapping the reins.

And with a pricking of one ear, my faithful steed eased out from the curb. I did not urge him into high, for I was totally unfamiliar with the controls. Besides, I told myself, the less conspicuous we were the better.

The neighborhood was showing signs of life. In one low-walled garden, an early athlete was swinging what looked like a nine-iron. We encountered several solitary women striding purposefully toward spots of domestic service, I thought. Several more cars swept by us, but we continued on our modest way—until, a block ahead, I saw a tall blue figure, trim and helmeted, looking, it seemed, in our direction. At that precise moment Hector, taking matters into his own mouth, swerved toward the pavement and came to a full stop.

Now I know that a policeman is a boy's best friend—particularly if the boy is lost in a great city. But it struck me that this officer must know the milkmen on his beat and was probably familiar with their customary stops. If he strolled my way—and no sooner had I thought it than he started strolling—he would wonder why I was stalled and proceed to inquire. He might even think it odd that the usual man was off and the substitute so young. I couldn't very well say, "My father left me here," or "Sorry, officer, but I'm escaping." It wouldn't sound normal.

Normal—that was it! I must make everything seem just as normal as possible. There could be only one reason why Hector had come to a stop—this address was a regular port of call, a well-known point of his daily route.

I looked into the back. One rack of full bottles gleamed white among the empties. I let the reins fall on the dash, picked up the loaded carrier, and whistling happily, dropped from the wagon. Out of the corner of my eye I saw that the law was now but half a block away.

With what I hoped was professional nonchalance, I opened the garden gate, walked up a gravel path, and deposited my cargo on the kitchen steps. Forcing myself not to hurry, I gathered up two empty pints and put them in the proper metal slots. When I re-opened the gate, the scene that met my eye was what I think they call bucolic. The guardian of law and order was standing at Hector's head engaged in a confidential conversation— with my horse!

Neither of them even turned around as, like Casey Jones, I mounted to the cabin. Then the animal-lover spoke.

It was a question. "Wullie's awee the dee?" (His accent was what we called at school "pure Morningsayde.")

I swallowed and said, "Ay." The policeman stepped back. I flapped the reins. And away we went, Hector and I, as calm and unarrested as anyone could wish.

We stayed that way as far as Clark Street, where, by my father's orders, we turned right and found ourselves in a considerable flow of morning traffic. At the jog where the street changed its name to Nicolson, I began looking for the sign of the "Faithful Friend." I was getting along surprisingly well with Hector, but I had no wish to take him into a congestion of cars and pedestrians.

41

There it was—an unimposing tavern, its sign in need of paint. And lounging outside of it, a rather dapper-looking individual in a white duster like my own. With gratifying skill, I persuaded Hector to park himself (though it's just possible that he was as used to this stop as to the others).

The white-coated gentleman advanced to my horse's head. Inside the wagon, I switched back to my raincoat. As my relief mounted to starboard, I dropped off to port. Under proficient management, Hector made a U-turn and trotted off, leaving me with the memory of a brief but beautiful friendship.

Even in summertime the Edinburgh mornings are apt to be nippy. By the time I reached the pub on Nicolson Street, a mass of gray clouds had obscured the western sky, and what had started as a clear day looked decidedly uncertain.

As far as I could tell, my father and I had gotten clean away from the inhabitants of the house where I had spent the night. No one had chased the wagon; no solitary cyclist had tagged along in our rear; no suspicious-looking persons stopped and stared at me. Nevertheless, I felt self-conscious as I tramped through the morning city. It occurred to me that a fugitive requires certain special skills; somewhere in a textbook on psychology I had read of people who imagined they were followed. They had my heartfelt sympathy. I must admit, too, a slight disappointment in my father's arrangements. A bus, no doubt, was better than a milk wagon, but neither vehicle quite came up to my idea of what the service might be expected to provide. Now an I-F Bluebird, for instance. . . .

But a bus it was. I had to wait for fifteen minutes, feeling every minute more conspicuous; but just as I began a fifth reading of the display posters outside Festival head-quarters, along came a one-four-four. For a variety of reasons I decided to sit upstairs. There were plenty of seats, and I took one on the near side. It was a very good thing that I did.

Most of the traffic, as was natural at that hour, was go-ing toward the city, and we bowled along at a pretty good clip. I paid my fare to Drumrinnoch, which I knew to be some five miles beyond Kirknewton. Near the Saughton jail we took on board two airmen and a woman with a market basket. Another stop, and three well-scrubbed children joined us. Still within the city, short of the Union Canal, we halted again. A queue of five men waited. Four sported caps and raincoats. But the fifth—I looked down at the top of a bowler hat worn above the wide shoulders of a dark-colored ulster. The man's left hand grasped a small black bag.

Impossible, I told myself. It could not be. But it was. With one foot on the platform of the bus, the bowler hat paused and looked up, scanning the top-deck windows. For an instant our eyes met. It was Dr. Fisher.

❊ 6 ❊

I could not be sure that he had spotted me, but it was idiotic to suppose that his boarding my bus—my bus of all available buses!—was coincidence. Breathlessly, I watched the head of the stairs.

A cap appeared. Another cap. Another. Their owners seated themselves astern and lighted cigarettes. The bus was under way again. But the bowler hat remained below.

Why shouldn't he? Unless I sprouted wings, there was no way for me to disembark except by descending—into his waiting arms. And if I somehow managed to get past him down below, he had only to follow me off, and I should lead him straight to my refuge.

If he ever allowed me to reach it!

I wracked my brains for possibilities. Maybe this was his regular morning route. Perhaps some wealthy invalid had haled him from the city. But why would he board a bus well out in the West End—and *my* bus, to boot? I still was not quite certain that he had recognized me in his upward glance; he might still be uncertain as to whether I had spotted him. But all he had to do was to sit and wait for me to move—and then take over.

I decided to make things easier for him.

It was raining now, and I turned up the collar of my "mac" and made my way below. The doctor was sitting well forward, apparently immersed in the *Scotsman* but keeping a weather eye on the driver's rear-view mirror.

Ignoring the conductor or guard or whatever they call him, I made for the front of the bus and addressed our chauffeur in the purest of American accents.

"Say," I said (in deference to British fiction), "this bus stops at a town called Dinwoodie, don't it?" I named a village that I knew to be several miles short of my destination.

The driver didn't bother to look around. "Ay," he assured me. "They'll call it out."

"Thanks loads," said I, and gazing over the passengers' heads at the advertisements above the windows, I made my way back to a vacant seat two behind the doctor. He appeared to be buried in his newspaper.

It was a pretty feeble gambit, but it might work. From all the doctor had seen of me, I wasn't a very bright lad; and if I had failed to notice him, I *might* be just stupid enough to make a public announcement of my destination. For the time being, I would let him wonder: either I had identified him—in which case my actions were extremely suspect—or I thought myself safely away and my questioning the driver was a star for him to steer by.

Westward we went. The rain came seeping down, not the big-drop-and-a-splash kind, but life in a cloud. Now and then the conductor called a stop. People got off. More people got on. Dr. Fisher-Finch found the *Scotsman* totally engrossing. But he never turned a page.

"Dinwoodie!" called the driver and the conductor at

once. As I rose, so did two or three others, and the doctor —whose reactions must have been excellent—swept past us in the aisle. He had decided, apparently, to play it straight and take me at my word. I had not seen him, and for reasons of his own, he was determined to be the first one off the bus. The others were already ahead of me as I sidled out of my seat, and the bus pulled to a rather tipsy halt at the edge of the high-crowned road. We stood in a swaying line—the doctor first, then the three intervening passengers, then me.

If Dr. Fisher-Finch had not been quite so cunning, my scheme would have fallen flat. As it was, he dismounted without turning round—having no wish for me to spot him. The three unknowns dropped off between him and the bus, and at the same instant I quietly resumed my seat. The conductor took a quick look for additional departures, saw none, and rang the bell.

With a lurch and a roar we were off; and looking back, I saw the bowler hat (now turned in our direction) standing in what I hoped was deep chagrin on the Dinwoodie pavement.

It is hard to say what moved me to get off at Kirknewton. Certainly not the weather, for the rain had thickened and the roadside was sloppy underfoot. (My father has explained to me since that I played in awfully good luck to get rid of the doctor as I did, and I suppose that my quitting the bus was another bit of the same.)

Anyway, I had sloshed along for barely half a mile when from somewhere behind me on the road I heard the unmistakable sound of a motorbike. I didn't turn to look—I knew! By ways and means unknown, my pursuer had procured himself another vehicle. I hoped there was nothing to distinguish the back of my raincoat from any other. However, for all that, I hugged the gray stone dike that edged the road.

But he neither stopped nor slackened. With the rippling chug that characterizes most British motorcycles, he was past me with a hiss and a splatter, the redoubtable bowler still firmly in place on his head.

I wondered just how safe I was. Undoubtedly, he would soon catch up with the bus. But then what? Would he ride ahead, ditch the bike, and resume his role of passenger? I hoped so. And as I hoped, up ahead and dimly red in the rain, I saw an Esso sign. Turn off at the gas station, the Boss had told me, and take the dirt road for—what was it?—oh yes, Plummet Lodge.

I advanced and reconnoitered. The gas pumps were idle and the filling-station doors were closed against the weather. In the outside phone booth a single bulb shone wanly into the dull morning. I skirted the building looking for a feeder roadway. Sure enough, taking off from the parking space at the rear of the station, a sandy lane led between walled fields. At the start of it a finger post carried two names, barely legible. "Bannock Leithen" was one, and "Plummet" was the other.

Pulling my collar up—the inner side of it was wet—I had gone about three steps when a familiar sound brought me to a standstill. The motorcycle was returning. Dr. Fisher-Finch must have caught the bus quickly and as quickly determined that it didn't carry anyone he cared about.

His engine slowed, putted, and came to a stop. The gas

station stood between him and me. I congratulated myself on not having asked directions and headed for the cover of some dripping trees.

But the bowler hat made no appearance, and in two or three minutes, I heard the bike kicked into action once again. The noise of its acceleration dwindled away toward Edinburgh, and I set out for Plummet Lodge.

The lane was soggy but by no means impassable. Someone with a biggish car used it frequently, for there were spacious ruts on either side. In the middle, the sandy surface was dented by multiple hoofprints.

After I had walked ten minutes, the wall on my left grew higher. A bit farther on I drew up before a pair of sizable wrought-iron gates. The lane continued ahead of me, but I knew that I had reached my objective, for suspended in the metal tracery that arched above the opening there was a plumb line with a hanging conic weight. The rain had stopped, and a flicker of sun cheered me on.

The gates were open, and I needed no further invitation. On my left was an unfenced field where two or three harmless-looking cows were peacefully grazing. To my right there was a forest of shrubbery. Forty or maybe fifty yards I went—when a bullet split the bushes on my right and thwacked into the gravel just in front of me.

7

Now I can't say that I have lived my life under fire—or
that I'm precisely an expert on ballistics—but this was no
spent shot. From the ripple it kicked up in the roadway, I
guessed at a .22 rifle. As it turned out, I was wrong about
the caliber. But while I stood stock still for a petrified instant, another slug came whining through the underbrush
and clonked into a stone six feet away.

There was no point in doing the prone bit. Both shots
had landed in the lane. Cover, I thought—the instincts of
my father's son coming into operation rather belatedly.
And since the only solid cover was an oak at the edge of
the pasture, I put it between me and the shooting as
quickly as I could.

Another slug quite literally bit the dust. All, mind you,
without a bang or a crack or any sort of decent rifle sound.
In so lonely a spot, it hardly seemed necessary for my as-
sailant to use a silencer.

But he was done with secrecy. A crashing in the bushes
heralded his approach, and I made myself as small as
possible behind the tree. Doubtless he thought he had got
me and was moving in for the gralloch, as the gutting of
a stag is known in Scotland.

Then, cool as you please in the misty morning air, a feminine voice sang out, "I say, there wasn't anyone really there, was there?"

It was a pleasant voice, neither squeaky nor gruff, and the accent was Miss Mitford's "U." But I couldn't have cared less. From fear, I had switched to anger, and I literally trembled with the indignation that is customary, I suppose, when you've been shot at by a female idiot.

Across the lane the bushes parted, and the criminal emerged. I must say she wasn't bad—barring the automatic in her brown right hand. I don't go in much for the so-called gentler sex, but this specimen was notably well assembled.

With some caution, I edged myself out from behind the tree. But before I could deliver myself of a just rebuke, another voice came out of the bushes behind her.

"Like I say—some square was in the picture. This-away!"

There is only one voice in Scotland that mingles a Clydeside brogue with "catty" conversation. Disregarding the girl, smoking weapon and all, I put my hands on my hips and shouted, "Grant! Tommy Grant, come out of those bushes and call off your gun-for-hire!"

He stumbled out of the shrubbery, and I never saw a more bewildered-looking youth. He even forgot his hep talk.

"My lady mother! It's Posy! Jonathan Flower—in the flesh!"

"The flesh," I said with all the dignity I could muster, "is almost too accurate a rendering. What, may I ask, are you doing here, and who is this female Deerslayer?"

It fitted pretty well, for she had on jodhpurs—which are a sort of leatherstocking, I suppose.

But she didn't apologize one bit. With Grant still properly aghast, she merely inquired—in a very cool way—"Are you the one Mother said might be coming?"

This was a bit of a baffler. For all I knew, her mother might have been expecting the minister. I realized that I was more bedraggled than impressive, and a spasm of embarrassment robbed me of my ordinary glibness. The only course was to play it on the strong side.

"I am looking," I said, "for a woman named Sophia."

The girl nodded knowledgeably. "Then you're the one. Mummy'll be home in a few minutes."

It seemed to me that I was entitled to a little more explanation. I pointed to Tommy. "I realize that this Grant character is capable of almost any kind of foolishness, but I was not aware that he went in for ambush. You may not know it, but I was very nearly scuttled."

She gave a low laugh, and believe me, these sixteen-year-old houris can sound sinister.

"We're teddibly soddy, of course. I've not had a chance to shoot since Daddy gave me the pistol, and when Tommy arrived with a silencer, we thought we might practice. You never know, you know."

I never did.

"It's so fearfully dismal to be doodly with a gun," she went on. And then, rather irrelevantly as I thought, "Future generations might be softened."

"Yes, I see," I said, thoroughly revolted.

Those Scots! Every four-year-old cleans his own shotgun; at six you start polishing the old man's elephant rifle;

your first bicycle is for Grand Prix purposes; and when you get yourself a car . . . ! Still, I rather liked her.

Her hair was in pigtails—an arrangement that I prefer to Italian mops and Kennedy puffs—but she was no mere infant. Even without the gun, there was in this young woman a lethal quality that could not be ignored.

"You'd best come up to the house," she said. "I'm Mary Hamilton, and I'm sure it's my mother you're meant to see."

At that instant there was a great crackling in the brush behind her, and a big brown mare "came whiffling through the tulgey wood." Aboard the beast was what I took to be a little girl, riding sidesaddle (even in Scotland you don't see that very often). Under her hard hat, her yellow hair settled down in a series of flops as the mare came to a reluctant halt.

"What-ho, you people!" I perceived that she was no little girl and learned a minute later that she was actually Mary Pigtail's mother—and my Sophia.

"You're Jonathan," she said. "I know. I know all about it. And your poor daddy. He's been having a time for himself, hasn't he? I've very precise messages for you—and I'm sorry to say they're not on the light side, exactly. Ah well"—she smacked the neck of the big horse with a friendly hand—ah well, we'll talk it over at the house. Come along then, people." She wheeled the mare into the roadway and was off at a canter.

There is nothing I like better than a biggish British lunch —except a biggish British tea. We had talked, and I had talked, and I had my orders from the Boss—apparently telephoned to Lady Hamilton earlier in the morning— when two beribboned housemaids laid a table in the rose garden and proceeded to produce a jingle of lobster, tongue, fresh peas, scones, and tea.

I was to be at the American Consulate in Edinburgh by half-past three that afternoon. Lady Hamilton was driving in for Tommy's sake to catch a train to the Highlands —and she would see me safely to the city. What I had to do at the Consulate was not disclosed, but my father had implied that I would be expected.

Lady Hamilton chatted on. "We're terribly fond of your father, Jonathan. He's not exactly a restful visitor, but—I don't know—he really does something for Plummet Lodge."

"Have you seen him this trip?" I asked.

"No, but he was here—let's see—ten months ago." I had been under the impression that ten months before he had been in China—but with the Boss, you never can be sure. "He was on one of his errands," she added. "I'm sure you have learned a great deal about them." She was obviously aware that his travels were not purely for pleasure.

I asked Tommy Grant where *he* was off to and discovered that he was headed for Inchdarroch to visit Alec Macnicol. He appeared to be much intrigued by my appearance at Kirknewton, but with extraordinary politeness for him, asked no questions. Neither did Lady Hamilton after her single reference to the Boss, but when she and Tommy went in to get ready for town, Mary Pigtail said to me, "I say, it must be wizard to have a father who's a courier! That's what he is, isn't he?"

Talk about feminine curiosity!

"It is indeed wizard," I told her.

She stuck out a very red tongue at me. (Her lips *are* very red for that matter, and without assistance, thank you.)

"Now you're going all mysterious on me," she protested.

"There are facts," I said, "which it is better not to know."

As the big blue Daimler rolled out the gate into the lane, I caught myself peering about for signs of my erstwhile pursuer. He may have been somewhere behind the dike, but if so, he kept himself well hidden. The Esso station at the highway had no customers. But when we had gone about a mile toward the city, I observed that a motorbike had picked us up and was following far astern. It stayed so very far back that I couldn't even tell whether its rider was a man or a woman. This fact in itself seemed to me suspicious—especially since Lady Hamilton, unlike most Scotswomen, drove rather slowly.

Mary caught me looking behind us.

"You keep turning around like an egg beater," she said elegantly. "I say, Mummy, are we being pursued?"

Lady Hamilton looked startled and gazed into the rear-view mirror. A dark red Jaguar had passed the motorcycle and was coming up fast.

"I hardly think so," she said. "After all, this road has considerable traffic."

"Golly, I hope we are," said Mary Pigtail.

"Cool, mon, cool," said Tommy Grant.

The Jaguar swept past us. In the far background, the motorbike came leisurely along. When we reached the city, I lost sight of it, and I don't really know to this day whether it had anything to do with my subsequent adventures.

Lady Hamilton parked the Daimler in Lothian Road, and we walked around the corner to Princes Street station. There had been, we discovered, a slight miscalculation. Tommy's train did not leave for another hour. The station clock said three-fifteen.

"I think I'd better leave you," I said. "I can take a taxi. The Consulate's on Regent Terrace, isn't it?"

"Right," said Lady Hamilton. "I don't remember the exact number, but they always fly an American flag over the door." She hesitated. "I hate to have you go alone, but I did promise to see Tommy off. You'll be right enough in a cab, I expect." She didn't know about my last taxi ride.

The rank was empty when we reached it, but almost at once a cab pulled up. I said good-by with many thanks to my attractive hostess, her gun-toting offspring, and T. Grant.

"If things ever get going as planned," I told Tommy, "I may see you in the Highlands yet. So long for now. The American Consulate on Regent Terrace, please." The driver touched his cap, and we were off into the traffic of Princes Street.

The standard interior of the cab was uncomfortably reminiscent, and I thought again of my ride of the night before.

Summer crowds are always strolling and gazing—in the Gardens and past the shops. I was rather surprised, however, to see an American flag displayed at the Overseas Club and another at the Royal Hotel. There was a third flying alongside the Union Jack at the North British. Suddenly, the reason for these displays overtook me. It was the Fourth of July, and Auld Reekie was saluting the American tourist trade.

We buzzed along past the Post Office and around the turn below Calton Hill. Nelson was smiling from his pinnacle, and the half-baked acropolis shone in the sun. From Regent Road we swung left into Regent Terrace. A pleasant street of noble houses, it smiles along a curve that looks on Holyrood. It is neither splendid nor ancient, but it speaks for that civility which talked with tolerance a century or so ago about the madness of the Middle Ages. The granite setts were smooth under our tires.

I looked for the flag that would mark the Consulate and spotted it almost at once. A bit further on, I saw another sample of the Stars and Stripes. The town was going Yankee with a vengeance—though from a doorway farther distant the tricolor of France vaunted a rival republicanism.

My cab pulled up at the first American flag; and, sure enough, hung on the door—rather informally, I thought—was a painted sign: U. S. CONSULATE.

The meter read three-and-six. I gave the man four shillings; he thanked me and proceeded to execute one of those amazingly tight turns that only British taxis can do. From the steps of the house, I watched his vehicular dexterity. The sunlight struck the gilt name letters on the taxi door. "G. L. Gillan," it said.

I don't mind telling you that my heart started to do some rather peculiar bits of pounding. I had ridden to my rescue apparently, with the very same cabbie who had as good as kidnapped me the night before. I remembered now his opportune appearance at the station. But wait—perhaps only the cab was the same. For Dr. Fisher-Finch's purposes, it might have been hijacked in off hours. After all, today's driver had brought me directly to my destination.

I looked at my watch. It said three-thirty on the nose. I looked at the house door. It said "214"—and on the painted sign, "U. S. Consulate." I looked up and down the street. A remarkable number of cars were at the curb, including a black Impala with what I recognized as a diplomatic license. Old Glory waved over my head as I yanked at the shiny brass bellpull.

The big door opened immediately. A man in a Marine sergeant's uniform seemed to be a combination of orderly and butler. Oddly enough, he bowed, and his deference struck me as faintly continental. So did his question.

"One wishes to see—?"

This isn't the usual approach from a leatherneck, but I paid it no mind.

"My name is Flower," I said. "I think the consul is expecting me."

"A moment and I will inquire."

The sergeant vanished into a darkish hallway and returned almost at once. "The consul," he said, "is in his office at the head of the stairs." He made a gesture, and I mounted a steep marble flight at the top of which a doorway waited—rather like a gaping mouth.

A man sat at a desk in silhouette against a tall French window. Back of him the sun picked out the traced wrought-iron of a balcony. I could not see the consul's face and had only an indistinct impression of bulk at the shoulders. The office door closed behind me.

"I believe, sir," I said, "that you are expecting me. I'm Jonathan Flower." As I spoke, my eyes got more accustomed to the light and shadow, and with his answer, in simultaneous shock, I heard the voice and saw the face of Dr. Fisher-Finch.

"Yes, my boy, we have been expecting you."

You've no idea what came into my mind. It was the sweetly solemn thought that they were having a bang-up tea at Plummet Lodge. For just the fraction of an instant, I could hear myself telling Mary Pigtail about my interview at the American Consulate.

But, as things stood, I didn't know what to say—and I didn't know what to do. It was possible that this man *was* actually the American consul and that I was involved in some fantastic mix-up in which nobody knew whose side was which. It was possible, but it wasn't very likely.

"What have you done with him?" I asked.

"Done with him? Done with whom?" Amazingly enough, he did sound American. A man of many parts, the doctor.

"With the consul, of course."

"My dear boy, I am the consul. Nor have you any reason to doubt it." His voice took on a note of menace. "You have come to me at your father's behest, have you not?" (I loathe people who say "have you not?".) "You will wish to remain with me for security."

"I'll wish no such thing, Dr. Fisher-Finch."

He laughed, and it was not a pleasant sound. "Very well

then, if you refuse to play the game according to my rules, we shall have to try other methods." His hand went to the drawer of the kneehole desk. Through the open window came the distant babble of voices—a garden party, perhaps.

"You are so refreshingly stupid," he said, "—a trait, I am sorry to say, that your esteemed father does not share. I was afraid that you would recognize our driver, but no— you walked gracefully into his arms. It occurred to me that the temporary nature of our door sign would arouse your suspicions. But no—you came gaily in. That sign, by the way, was put in place a minute before your arrival and, of course, was removed the instant you entered the house. As for the flag, what more natural for summer tourist tenants on the Fourth of July? Perhaps you saw the other one some doors away? It is flown by the actual consul of your precious nation." He indulged himself in another phlegmy chortle.

"I like to do things this way," he said. "I like to play upon the dullness of the average brain. Some of my colleagues are doubtless more direct. But"—his wide shoulders shrugged—"of what value is open violence on the street when a little thought, a little planning, a little subtlety can accomplish the same end without disturbance?

"Besides," he went on, "as things stand, we do not want your life. We merely want *you*."

He rose to his feet, and I saw that in his hand he held a hypodermic syringe.

There wasn't much time for thinking. Maybe I might have managed things much better. It occurred to me, however, that the conversational phase of our interview had gone on long enough.

I squatted. That's all you could call it: I dropped in a crouch, jammed my shoulder into the kneehole opening, and heaved the desk directly at the doctor. I followed it up as it caught him—at about the middle of his thighs— and he went over backward with the desk on top of him.

There was no time, I felt, to examine his bruises. Instead, I popped through the window onto the balcony. It ran almost the length of the block, with dividers between each house.

The dividers didn't delay me. I took the first one to the right side like a hurdle and looked down. A good sixteen feet. Not for me. It *might* be done, but I had had a little experience with an overall drop of somewhat less—at one of my New England boarding schools—and I was not eager.

Thankfully, I observed that the next house farther on had an extruded drainpipe. From below, in the garden of the house I had reached, came the same muddled hubbub of conversation I had heard before. I had no time to look down. Instead, I straddled the railing, grabbed at the drainpipe, and slithered merrily to earth.

I found myself in multiple company. It was indeed a garden party—and the garden, to my horror, was walled —a sizable rectangle with the house at my end and a gate at the other.

Two fancy umbrellas were up over tea tables, and around each table a cluster of males ogled a gaggle of girls. For the moment, nobody appeared to have noticed my sudden descent, and I hung close to the wall of the house. I thought of the back door, but if I had used it, it would have led me back through the house to the street. And my experience of Scottish gardens led me to believe that the gate was almost certainly locked.

As to costume, I might have been worse off. A number of the men were in blazers and flannels. I ventured to skirt the left-hand flowerbeds when I heard someone say, "Who's the lad?"

On I went to the back wall. I tried the gate, and as I had supposed, it was locked. A number of people at the nearer tea table were now staring in my direction, but no one had yet appeared on the balcony of the pseudo consulate.

The garden wall was at least nine feet high. But by one of the tea tables I had spotted a bamboo pole leaning against the stonework. Heaven knew why it was there, but it looked reasonably stout and was certainly long enough. Unfortunately, it was perched directly behind the chair of an elderly and rather severe-looking dowager. I decided to brave the issue.

Strolling casually up to the tea table, I put on my best British accent and said, "I do hope you'll forgive me—I shan't put you out for more than a moment, but Grandmother needs the pole." I pointed at the desired object. (After all, I thought, people do have grandmothers, and some grandmothers probably need poles—at least from time to time.)

The dowager lifted a glance whose iciness lacked only a lorgnette.

"Pole?" said she—as if I were suggesting an international incident. "What pole, boy?"

"Right there," I said, pointing again. "She uses it to roll up carpets, you know." I was getting nervous. The pseudo consulate was sure to be in pursuit soon.

The group around the table eyed me questioningly,

but one nice chap with an O.U.L.T.A. (Oxford University Lawn Tennis Association) badge on his jacket cut in behind the dragon's chair and managed to move her a bit.

I reached the pole. (All this had taken less than a minute.) My hosts and hostesses, I felt, deserved a word of parting cheer.

I grabbed the stick, remembering the rules—left hand top, right hand bottom—and with a cry of "Criadh Mor!" I launched myself at a gallop for the back wall, planted the foot of the pole a decent distance away, and sailed over the barrier in a reasonably horizontal vault.

I don't think I really disturbed the party, though I can believe that the dowager said something—"How odd!" probably.

I found myself in a kind of private park. A number of the older terraces and crescents, as I knew, maintained these cooperative bits of landscape to which only the local householders had access. The park behind Regent Terrace was unusually attractive. Nestling under the shadow of Calton Hill, its walks were pleasant, its trees considerable, and its lawns well tended.

Crossing a path that fed the back gate of the terrace gardens, I broke through some brush and came on a broad expanse of fresh-cut turf. The field was scarcely flat, but an impromptu soccer match was going on, three players against four—all of about my age. My recent exertion had left me a little out of puff, so I stood and watched for a bit. On a wild kick the ball came near me, and I booted it back to the players. One of the three-man side called, "Take a hand, Jock! We're the neediest."

It struck me that I had nowhere to go except perhaps to the real American consulate. Leaving the neighborhood wouldn't help, and to linger a while with these athletes might serve to conceal me as an individual and at the same time keep open a line of possible contact.

The boys were all from the Royal High School and, like me, just through for the summer. For the best part of an hour we kicked and ran—while I, of course, kept a wary eye in the direction of Regent Terrace and gave more than a single glance at the few strollers who appeared on the garden paths.

Sweaters on the grass at each end of the oval field served as goals. Whichever player happened to be nearest them served as goalie. When I entered the game, the score was 2-1 in favor of our opponents. Ten minutes later we were down 4-2. Ten more minutes, and despite my frequent looks about, I had observed no signs of pursuit.

The biggest of us was a chap named Stuart, who dribbled exceedingly well, controlled the ball finely, and was lightning fast. (In my opinion he may very well play some day for Scotland.)

He started down the field on my side—we were playing two up and two back. Swerving abruptly and executing an intricate Charleston with his feet, he diddled my forward completely and came thundering on at me. He was too good to tackle with any certainty of success, and I decided to race him for the goal. I reached the space between the sweaters some forty feet ahead of him when he let loose a looping drive that went way over my head and kept bounding—down a slope, across one path, and on toward another, where a nursemaid was calmly wheeling a pram.

The ball had nearly stopped when I caught up with it —right beside the nursemaid. She was apparently a very coolheaded female, for she had seen the kick and, as we sometimes say in the States, had paid it no mind.

I scooped up the ball and said, "I'm awfully sorry we came so close to you."

Her answer jarred my solar plexus.

"It's quite all right, Master Flower."

I had hardly glimpsed her face, but now she turned. To my utter dismay, it was Mrs. McGregor, my prison wardress of the night before.

"Be a good lad," she said, "and help me tuck the baby in."

Like a sleepwalker under hypnosis, I advanced on the pram. Except for the usual afghans and sheets, it was tenantless; and where the baby's head would ordinarily be— under the shelter of the hood—lay a neatly printed card.

WILL MEET YOU YOUR ROOM AT SCHOOL LATE TEA HASTA LUEGO BOSS

The nursemaid spoke very softly. "Be a good lad and do's ye're told. Away with you now and back to your game."

With what Mr. Francis Thompson calls "deliberate speed, majestic instancy," she resumed her calm perambulation.

To my football companions, I had merely been apologizing for a near miss. For myself, I had never had my head spun so dizzily.

I booted the ball back to our ground and followed it, asking myself a hundred questions. My concentration on the game fell off noticeably, and in the succeeding quarter of an hour the opposition scored three goals.

What on earth was this? Was I being lured to my doom outside the city? Was the message another hoax, or had my father somehow kept track of my whereabouts? But how —how could he have traced me from the counterfeit consulate? Whose side was Mrs. McGregor really on? And if I dismissed the pram note, what then? Where was I expected to go?

Gradually, the issue boiled itself down to two possibilities. If I chose to believe that the message was trap bait, it followed that the rather likable Mrs. McG. was purely and simply an enemy agent and that all kinds of skulduggery waited at school—if I were fool enough to accept their invitation. On the other hand, if the note were genuine, then Mrs. McGregor had probably been instrumental in my escape from the "safe" house and might very well have slipped me the data on the milkman. The lady puzzled me; somehow it was hard to think of that kindly, pink-cheeked Scotswoman as "Mrs. McGregor, counterspy."

Unlikely items sometimes make up your mind for you. In my case it was the "hasta luego" bit. It had been used in the bogus telegram. But the enemy must know by now that I knew that telegram to have been bogus. Were they so naïve as to suppose that I would accept it readily as genuine code from the Boss? Would they count on it to work twice? Or wouldn't they rather—in sending me another message—stay away from a phrase that had already proven undependable? And mightn't my father's mind be working just as mine was—count on the calculating logic of the ungodly and work with the whimsey of the Flowers?

By the time we shook hands all around over the soccer ball and the "jolly goods" and "good shows" were said and done, I had made up my mind. I would take a chance on the genuineness of the baby-cart communiqué and head for school—but with my eyes peeled for the slightest sign of treachery.

The boys went over the hill toward the Royal High School from which, I surmised, the football might have been borrowed. I was fortunate enough to find an unlocked gate in the far side of the gardens and let myself out without difficulty.

I felt it necessary, of course, to skulk. By this wonderful word I mean that I was in a collar-turned-up, fugitive frame of mind, pivoting frequently on my way to Leith Walk to look behind and about for the doctor or his minions. One glance behind revealed a fat man in a bowler hat —but he turned into a pub called the "Golden Goose," and I saw him no more.

Again I chose the upper deck of the bus and watched the riders on the beach at Portobello. The giant swimming pool was white with artificial surf, and thousands of people were taking the sun along the shore—though the sun wasn't doing so well as a matter of fact, and a cloud mass was coming on from the west. Nobody disturbed my bus ride, and as far as I could see, nobody was particularly interested in it.

I dismounted opposite Lavendar House and walked to the school gate. I had intended to go straight to MacDuff's cottage (for the chances were that my room had been stripped and locked during the day), but the first person I saw was Clammy Krohten, our refugee language master. He has a Ph.D. from Göttingen and a face like a tired turnip.

He was standing by the roadside as if he were expecting someone—probably by car and perhaps unfamiliar with the grounds. His surprise at seeing me, however, was without affectation.

"What's this, Flower? I thought you had left."

"I did, sir; I'm just back to pick up some things." I remembered that, in a way, he had been in on the beginning of my recent adventure, and I wondered whether it would be wise to mention the telegram. Little as I liked him, he was, after all, a master and presumably had some responsibility for the welfare of his students.

"That wire you gave me turned out to be inaccurate," I told him.

"Indeed? And how so?"

"It told me to take off and meet a friend of my father's in Edinburgh, and it was signed by my—it was signed the way my father would sign it."

"But your father was here last night. He was pointed out to me. I myself saw him."

"Yes, sir. He never sent the telegram at all. It was—"

"A stupid joke, no doubt." He didn't seem to wonder where I had spent the night. "What is it that you have come back for? What do you expect to find?"

He had me on that one. I had no idea.

"My climbing boots," I said as casually as I could. "Do you know, sir, whether my room has been knocked down —cleaned out, that is?"

"No. I would not know this." He seemed to be thinking hard and looking me over very carefully at the same time. "Your housemaster is gone," he said. "Have you seen anyone here at school—MacDuff, for example?"

I told him no, and his flaccid face was wreathed in smiles.

"So then, no one knows you are here—except myself,

that is? Well, come along then. I have a key to your house. We shall go and see if your things are all in place. Then, if you like, we shall have tea together. I believe that all the other boys are gone."

We were walking down the hundred-yard straightaway that separates a number of the school buildings. I couldn't suppress my dislike for Clammy, but after all, he was going out of his way to be decent. Somehow or other I had to substantiate my interest in the boots, and his key to the house was as good as anyone's. MacDuff appeared nowhere; the quad was empty; and except for a faint light in the chapel, the place was lifeless. Few spots are as lonely as a school once the holidays have started.

I considered telling Mr. Krohten that I was expecting my father. Then I thought better of it. I had no fears that the Boss would not find me—as long as I was on the school grounds and provided Mrs. McGregor's note was honest.

10

We stopped at the door of the house, a black rectangle in a tawny stucco wall, with slim windows like arrow slits on either side. Clammy produced a formidable bunch of keys. The downstairs hall was dark in the late afternoon, and I pressed the switch at the foot of the stairs; but the current had already been cut off.

The school is not a very old one—as public schools go— but electrical eccentricity is the right and privilege of every British institution built before World War I. We had our own plant and generator, and a sudden curtailment of service was by no means unusual. Krohten's voice came from the shadows behind me. "There is light enough for what we have to do."

Somewhat unnecessarily, as I thought, he followed me up the stairs, but alas, the room door was locked, and I had dutifully left my key at the porter's lodge the night before.

"It is unfortunate," said the language master. "I have no keys for the individual rooms."

It occurred to me that there had been something suspiciously like a master key on that big bunch of his. (In point of fact, I could easily have picked the lock and had done so a number of times—in emergency—but not with Clammy Krohten looking on.)

"I'll have to get MacDuff," I said.

"That will be difficult for a little while." The master's voice was oddly thick. "I happen to know that he is at Gullane. He is an old friend of the golf professional there, so I hear." He coughed. "I am certain he will return soon. Meanwhile, why not some small tea in my rooms? I should be pleased—"

He sounded as if he meant it, and because there is always a soft spot in my heart for people who seem lonely —and because I didn't know what on earth else to do—I said, "Thank you very much, sir. That sounds splendid."

We walked together across melancholy vacancies. Clammy had rooms in one of the small cottages—he wasn't made to be a housemaster, I thought—on the far edge of the school complex. His sitting room was alarmingly tidy —not an open book nor an out-of-place cushion. No pipes or tobacco, no chair-draped flannels, no dirty tennis shoes. In other words, a room to rouse precaution rather than respect. A door to our left was shut, but he opened another that gave on a tiny pantry. He lit a burner under the kettle and brought out tea things—a jar of jam and some rather dreary-looking biscuits.

"If you want to wash up," he said, "the bathroom is through there." He pointed. I did and went, remembering to shut both bedroom and bathroom doors behind me as you always do in Scottish households to conserve the heat —even in summer. Coming back after a moment or two, I startled him. Or perhaps it was the mighty music of the flushing mechanism—though he ought to have been used to that.

At any rate, as I came into the room, he had poured the tea, and his hand was poised above my cup in a way that immediately aroused my suspicion. His hand dropped to his side, and he stared at me over his shoulder with a very odd look on his face.

"You were quick," he observed, and he didn't sound as if he were very pleased about it.

I made some conversation. "You have better water pressure than we do at the house." The roar of flushing was still audible behind me.

He nodded and seemed to relax a little. "Yes, but the plumbing is poor. Will you have milk in your tea?"

I don't, as a rule, but I noticed that there was already milk in *his* cup.

"Yes, thank you," I said. My one idea was that those cups must look alike, for I could think of no better insurance move than to stall and somehow attempt that ancient stratagem, the switcheroo.

He poured the milk. I stirred in some sugar and lazily spread a biscuit. How was I going to get him out of the room? I bit into my biscuit and stirred again. Then came inspiration, straight from the plumbing, where Niagara still foamed.

"That thing makes quite a noise, doesn't it?" I spoke mildly and hoped he did not think me impolite.

He rose like a hungry trout. "I will fix it. There is a thing that has to be jiggled." He went through the bedroom door, leaving it partly open, and in thirty seconds the torrent ceased to be in spate. But even before it was silenced, the teacups had changed places.

"It is a curious thing to me," he said as he sat down again, "how the English people can tolerate mechanical inefficiency. The possibility of greater convenience simply does not occur to them." He took a deep draught of tea. "On the continent this sort of thing, minor irritation though it is, would never be allowed. Nor in America, of course."

He was watching me, and I was watching him.

"Why cahn't the English teach their children how to plumb?" I asked. The parody was lost on him.

"Eh? Yes. Exactly so. Will you have another cup? Oh, not quite ready? Well, drink up. There is more, as you say, where this came from."

It was a weird situation. If he *had* put something in my tea, there was no way for me to know how long it would take to act or what the nature of its effect might be or even whether it was lethal. I doubted this last possibility. What was it Fisher-Finch had said at the consulate? "As things stand, we do not want your life; we merely want you." Provided things still stood, I was probably not embarking on the career of a poisoner.

Meanwhile, he chatted on, all the while observing me with what I thought was growing intensity. I had a second cup and so did he.

"I am afraid that the amenities of a deserted school are not extensive," he remarked.

"Oh, I'm doing fine, sir," I assured him. It seemed to me that he breathed in quickly. "May I have a third cup, sir?"

"Of course," he said. "I will get more hot water." He picked up the pot from the table and disappeared into the pantry. There's no reason for *him* to want any more, I told myself—so he'll dose the whole batch this time.

"I will make it a little stronger," he announced. I could

not see him, but I heard him pouring. "This tea has an unusual bouquet, do you not—"

His voice broke off with a kind of snarl. In the same instant there was the sound of breaking crockery, and a great weight crashed to the floor, shaking the house. Mr. Krohten lay still across the pantry door.

He had fallen backward and lay with one hand above his head as if to ward off an impending blow. His breathing was heavy, but he had not lost color. I nudged him with a tentative foot, but he was wholly lost to consciousness. Remembering some of my lighter reading, I knelt and pulled back one of his lids. His eyes were rolled up, the pupils out of sight. I didn't know whether that was good or bad. But I was glad I had switched the teacups. Or had he had a stroke?

The telephone rang, a knife in the silence.

My first inclination was to let it ring. Then it occurred to me that perhaps there was a chance of learning something—either about the enemy or about Krohten himself. I decided to impersonate my host.

"Hello," I said, trying to copy his intonation.

The voice at the other end was deep, with a decidedly Teutonic accent. "Van Hoost here."

The name rang a bell. "Yes," I said. "Any more post cards from Copenhagen?"

A sputtering came over the wire. "You fool—not on the phone!" Then silence. Then, "You have the boy?"

"No."

"But we know that he went—he was observed at the gates."

I couldn't resist. Resuming my usual voice, I asked, "By

74

whom, old friend? Was it Finch or Fisher or merely Mrs. McGregor?" (I found out later that I did Mrs. McGregor an unintentional favor by linking her with the known enemy. They had grown slightly suspicious of her allegiance.)

"Who is this?" The deep voice was furious.

"Sherlock Holmes," I answered.

The line went dead.

My host had begun to snore. I had no idea what to do for him, but I took a pillow from the bedroom and placed it under his head. He looked more comfortable, but it did nothing, apparently, for his state of mind.

Despite the jam and biscuits, I was terribly hungry, and though prudence warned me to quit the premises, prudence was never one of my favorite girls. I found a tin of smoked pheasant—on reserve, I presume, for a really fancy tea—and polished off the lot. I wondered when and how my father would show up—and whether MacDuff were back from Gullane (unless that had been a lie)— and what I should say about Mr. Krohten.

Again the phone rang.

"Two-twenty-one-B Baker Street," I said.

It was van Hoost again. "Am I speaking, as I think, to Jonathan Flower?"

"As you think," I said.

"What are you doing in the place where you are—where you have no business to be? Is your father with you?"

"If he were, I wouldn't tell you. But since he isn't, I may say that he's headed in your direction." After all, a gambit's a gambit. "As for what I'm doing, it's more or less up to you. Your friend Krohten, at this moment, is standing about eight feet from the business end of my pistol. If you or any of your charmers disturb me—"

"We are coming. You would not dare—"

"Oh, wouldn't I though? One glimpse of you in the school grounds, and—"

"We are coming." He had hung up.

Well, I supposed they were, and I pondered my next move. More or less out of curiosity, I rolled Mr. Krohten partly over. He showed no signs of animation, but the jingle from his trousers reminded me that I had keys to the situation practically in hand.

I possessed myself of the instruments, locked the unprotesting master in his chambers, and departed across the school grounds to the gymnasium.

It had started to rain, and the deserted walks were darker than they would normally have been at that time of year. I let myself into the gym and tried a wall switch. If MacDuff were back and came to investigate, so much —from my point of view—the better. But the power was still off.

Fortunately, I knew my way pretty well and had no trouble through the gathering murk in getting downstairs to the gun room. The special lock that I knew was on that door gave me pause, but after trying three keys that looked like possibles, I hit the mark with a fourth and entered our academic arsenal.

Its stock was not impressive. There were four or five reasonably handy shotguns, a couple of fine Purdys belonging to the Head, and thirty or forty Belgian rifles, single-shot and relics of 1914. There were no pistols.

A 12-gauge over-and-under was my selection. (It struck

me as a good sort of discourager, and, after all, I was not out for puma—or so I thought.) From the cartridge cabinet I borrowed—mark the word—a dozen proper shells. Then I headed back for the house.

If they were really coming to get me, I reasoned, they would head first of all for Krohten's rooms. They had talked to me there on the telephone, and for all they knew, I was, as I had said, still holding him at gun point. Moreover, there came into my mind the picture of those firing slots on each side of the house door, and I thought that if the business came to an actual siege, I would be better off there than trying to barricade the door of Mr. Krohten's rooms.

Besides, I had had about enough of Mr. Krohten. I was no longer worried about his health, present or eventual, but I was weary of his inert form.

They must have called from fairly nearby, for as I fumbled for the house key—somewhat handicapped by my weapon—I heard a car grate to a stop on the gravel drive outside the porter's lodge. Was it MacDuff, I wondered? And if not, *where* was MacDuff? I looked at my watch; nine o'clock, it said. I put it to my ear—the silly thing had stopped.

I found the key and let myself into the now wholly dark hall. My pen-sized flashlight was enough to load the gun by, and having checked it, I pushed open one of the arrow-slot windows—they were casements—and took station. While I could not see the porter's lodge nor the buildings near the chapel, I enjoyed a good view of the school's central portion and of Mr. Krohten's abode. From the latter, lighted windows glistened on the wet.

77

As I watched, a dark figure moved from the shadows into the modest pool of light. Nothing about the man aroused a sense of recognition; but I was reasonably sure I knew the shape that followed him. Squat and sturdy, wide and bowler-hatted, the doctor was walking with a limp tonight—rather like someone whose legs had been bruised by sudden contact with a solid object. A third man appeared, shorter even than the doctor. The troops were out, but their movements appeared to be a little uncertain.

They fumbled with the cottage doorknob. Or so it seemed to me at sixty yards' range. I tried to remember whether the outside lock of the small residence had been complex or simple. I had no clear recollection.

But it probably wouldn't have mattered anyway, for now one of them was kneeling in front of the door and applying, I assumed, some lock-picking instrument.

The door opened, and the doctor disappeared inside, accompanied by the first of the three visitors. They would probably have little trouble with the inner entry to Krohten's rooms. The third man lingered in the shadows just beyond the patch of light—a sentinel, obviously. Lights came on in the upstairs hall.

For the thousandth time that day, I wondered what I ought to do. There was still no sign of my father, and I was growing surer and surer that the pram message was just another trap. Perhaps it would be wisest to get away at once, back to the city, out to the country—anywhere.

The least I could do was to establish a line of retreat. I propped the shotgun against the corridor wall, and shielding my small torch with one hand, I made my way to a back window, unlocked it, and left it halfway open.

No sooner had I returned to my observation post than the door of Krohten's cottage opened and, in the gathering gloom, Dr. Fisher-Finch and his friend joined their third crony and appeared to engage in a heated discussion.

Apparently agreed upon a plan (I learned later that they had managed to revive the sleeping master and had been urged by him in my direction), they advanced toward the house and me.

Twenty feet short of my doorway stockade, they stopped. The doctor spoke in a low but carrying tone.

"You—young Flower—we know where you are. Come out or we are coming in."

The sensible thing was to keep perfectly quiet. They had no sure way of knowing where I was. What with their somewhat shaggy pursuit, I might have left for foreign parts immediately after scragging Krohten.

For once, I did the sensible thing.

"Flower, this is the last warning." The doctor had something metallic in his hand, and I didn't like the look of it.

I did the thing that wasn't sensible at all.

"Come one step nearer," I told them through the window slit, "and I'll be forced to blow your toes off. Toes first, then heads."

"Why you—" Snarling, the man next to the doctor came bravely, if hesitantly, on. One step.

I fired at the ground in front of him, and the house hallway rocked with thunder.

There was absolute silence for a moment. Then, weirdly, the sound of mighty organ music swept the deserted campus. I realized at once that it came from the chapel, the doors of which someone had opened. It was a standard hymn tune, played with full diapason chorus. In the thick of this curious battle, the words came to me instantly:

> "Fight the good fight
> With all thy might . . ."

The enemy appeared to be transfixed. The thought occurred to me that they were oddly susceptible to religious influence. Then I saw that the third man had been hit. A pellet had bounced off the pavement in front of him and caught him in the leg. He was clutching his trouser and beginning a slow spin. The other two had him by the elbows.

Boom, boom-boom, boom went the organ:

> "Christ is thy strength
> And Christ thy right . . ."

I wasn't sure that the recitalist knew of my situation, but he was certainly ministering to my need.

Dr. Fisher-Finch had apparently made up his mind that things no longer "stood as they had"—for he raised his hand and a whining bullet buried itself in the wall behind me.

I fired back—a little closer to them this time—and they dispersed, running together in the direction of the porter's lodge, where darkness and distance gave them perfect cover. There they could linger till I made a move. Thence they could scatter to surround my fortress.

❖ 11 ❖

I had gained a moment's respite, but it wasn't a nice situation. I was tense and tired. Never before in my life had I so much as pointed a loaded gun at a living person. It was one of the rules of our bachelor ménage and one which was prerequisite to using guns at all. If, a few moments before, I had aimed a little higher, evil as the foe might be—it was not pleasant thinking.

The organist had changed his tune, unbothered by my blasts. I tried to take stock of the situation. My father had not appeared. MacDuff, the porter, must have been detained at Gullane or perhaps halted by the three musketeers on his return to school. Aside from them and me, the only living creature in the grounds appeared to be the impervious ass at the organ, blaring gospel ditties into the murderous night. . . . What was he playing now?

It was one of those jazzy revival songs that are being borrowed by hillbilly crooners. I remembered the lyric:

> "O come to the church in the wildwood,
>   O come to the church in the dale:
>   No spot was so dear to my childhood
>   As the little brown church in the vale.
>   O come, come, come—"

Et cetera. Absolutely mad.

Or was it?

Suddenly I caught on. Somebody was giving orders to somebody—by organ. "Fight the good fight. . . . Come to the church." If what I guessed were true, it must be time for Jonathan Flower to check out of his stronghold and repair to the chapel.

I had sense enough to break the gun before crawling through my open back window. As it was, the barrel hit the sash.

The night was thoroughly wet and had arrived at that state of pale darkness which is about as far as it goes in the summer in Scotland. The organ was playing something quieter and more melodious. I had heard it before, but it did not immediately bring definite words to mind. I hoped I wasn't missing any valuable information.

With a wary glance in the direction of the porter's lodge —now a dark mass against the sky—I skirted the back of the house and crept on behind Robinson's. Like all the halls, this one was dark, but from the far corner of the building, I could see the Gothic shape of light that was the chapel door.

Still the music played, and still the rain came down, driving southeast from across the Forth. My danger point, I realized, was a silhouetted entering of the chapel itself. The maniac musician might be poison, but I had a strong feeling that he (or she) was on my side. The doctor had apparently declared a shooting war. "Things" did not stand as they had stood. Or perhaps he had simply had a temper tantrum. "We do not want your life; we merely want you."

I ran, zigzagging a bit (in what I hoped was a baffling pattern), and made the dark at the side of the chapel. Then, gun and all, I charged the lighted opening, keeping as close as I could to the jamb. . . . Once through, I skittered into a pew at the right.

The school chapel is a pleasant, quiet place. Without flamboyance, it makes past and present meet. World War II added a lot of memorials, of course, but on the whole the Boer business and 1914 seem to predominate.

"To the glory of God," I read, "and in memory of Lt. Hector McKewn, R.F.C., Ypres"—and the date. The "R.F.C." dated it sufficiently.

"Dulce et decorum est"—my scansion was bad—"pro patria mori."

All this in dim light while the organ kept on with its pleasant, moderated music. A single lamp lighted the chancel and colored the polychrome plaques.

I said a little prayer and walked up the aisle. Two steps mounted to the choir, behind which the organ was placed crosswise, so that its operator faced the altar. I saw his back —a medium-sized man in a great white surplice with split sleeves. His concentration on the music was admirable.

Close behind him as I was, I could read the title of his score. It was Brahms' arrangement of "Welcome, welcome, dear Redeemer." On the console shelf to his right lay a Smith and Wesson .38 revolver. He turned, and it was my father's voice that said, "Happy to have you aboard, old boy.

"Job one is over," he continued. "The next thing to do is to get out of this *abbaye de Thélème*."

He scooped up the tails of his surplice, disposed some-

how of the Smith and Wesson, and switched off the organ.
Then, abruptly, before the air could gasp into too strange
a gargle, he flicked it on again.

"Have to say good night," he said. "Let's see—'Abide
with me' won't do. No. I have it—'Now the Day Is Over' "
—and to the strains of that comforting lullaby he gave his
hands and feet, precisely as if he were playing at a routine evensong.

"There. Perhaps that will quiet their restless souls," he
said, "but I doubt it."

He poured the organ's richness into a Dresden Amen
and switched off the overhead light.

"It is time, I think, to be going."

"But where, Boss?"

"Like this."

He slid off the bench and led me—to all intents and
purposes by the hand—to a door leading off the choir,
through a tiny sacristy, into the wet night.

Behind the chapel was a small MG—bucket seats, lights
off.

"We can talk as we go," he told me. "The situation has
changed completely. And, I may say, very much thanks to
you."

We took off with a minimum of starting snort in the
direction of Edinburgh.

I kept still for a bit. Then, "Excuse me," I said, "but
may I ask why you had to sit and play the organ while I
battled unto death?" (There are these contretemps—even
in the best-regulated families.)

"Ask away. I had every confidence in your ability to
handle the situation."

"Thank you very much. But if I hadn't found you—"

"You were bound to find me. I knew you were in the house because I saw you go in, gun and all. When I heard your shot, I realized that they had arrived and that you were exhibiting competence. Their pistol fire disturbed my music, but I know them for what they are; and when you blazed away a second time, I could picture their panic. 'How are the mighty fallen, and the weapons of war perished!'"

We must have been quite a sight to the ordinary motorist on the Portobello Road. The Boss had not bothered to rid himself of his surplice, and it flew out behind him, soggy in the rain but gallant as a banner—and this all the way back to Edinburgh.

Meanwhile, we talked.

"I'm sure you had a good lunch at Plummet?"

"I did indeed"—and I told him about the encounter with Mary Pigtail and Tommy Grant.

"And Sophia," he asked, "how is she?"

"In excellent form, I should say. She was terribly nice and quite worried, I think, when they put me in the taxi."

"Our friends are clever at times. Getting that driver into the rank at exactly the right moment—"

"But I should have recognized the name on the cab," I insisted.

"You should have recognized the phony character of the false consulate." He stopped talking and shifted down to round a sharpish curve. "I will admit that the fact of its being the Fourth of July gave them an unusual opening for monkeying about with flags. Fortunately, I had a friend on the Terrace."

"With a baby carriage, perhaps?"

"It might be."

I knew enough not to push my inquiry too far, but I had one burning question.

"Who *are* these birds? May I know that much?"

My father's surplice whipped and cracked in a plume of splendor. The wind and the rain drove at our faces.

"Holland," said the Boss, "is a curious country well known for its neutrality."

" 'The rain,' " I said, " 'falls mainly in the plain.' "

He ignored my comment. "Holland, as I say, is well known for its consistent policy of neutralism. During World War II, this tradition was broken. The Dutch behaved themselves with great courage and determination and suffered unimaginable losses."

"I know."

"But in Holland, as in all other countries, there are men whose selfish interests twist them away from a proper national—or international—attitude. Nine-tenths of the world's illicit trade in diamonds centers around Amsterdam. The Hague is headquarters not only for treaty making but also for treaty selling. For every legitimate diplomat in the Netherlands, there are four undercover agents. Some are Dutchmen; many are men without a country; and the interests they serve may be healthy for the rest of us or quite the reverse. Considering the way you've spent this particular glorious Fourth, I suppose you know that there's a man named—"

"Van Hoost," I broke in.

"Yes. And while I've tangled from time to time with enemy agents"—I knew he was speaking mildly—"I have never known a more unscrupulous or detestable character."

I thought it best not to ask for Mijnheer van Hoost's specific ambitions. The Boss filled me in—a little bit.

"The man is superbly egotistical. His confidence in himself leads him into all kinds of absurd bypaths. He thinks his way of doing things is subtler and cleverer than anybody else's way. He speaks twelve languages—in every sort of dialect. And his nerve is colossal."

"I believe," I said, "that I have met him."

We had reached the city and were keeping well away from the center of things. To my surprise, the Boss pulled up at one of those insurance offices on George Street that were once handsome town houses.

With total aplomb, his surplice notwithstanding, he produced a key and let us into what appeared, from the outside, to be an empty office. But empty it was not.

I have never had such service and attention. There was, indeed, an office front. That is to say, the two large rooms facing the street were equipped with desks, phones, typewriters, and the usual impedimenta of a business establishment. At the end of the central corridor, however, there was a sort of second front door. The Boss played a tune against it with his fingers, and it was opened almost immediately by a houseman in a gray jacket with striped lapels and cuffs.

"Good evening, Mr. Five. And you too, sir." He made me a small bow—suitable, no doubt, for Mr. Five's juvenile guest. "This way, gentlemen. Will it be for the night, or shall you want the private flat for an extended time? I may say, sir, that we expect the General—Mr. Three, that is—on Wednesday."

"Just for tonight, Parker. Thank you very much."

We were led into a comfortably fitted bed-sitting room.

"We could do with some sandwiches and tea. And I'd appreciate it if you'd lose that MG that we came in. Have someone drop it off at Bruntsfield Links, will you?"

Parker was running a bath in the adjoining dressing room and laying out towels. "Very good, sir." He came out of the bathroom, smiling at us both, the image of hospitality. "Anything to drink, sir?"

"A small whisky for me." My father is very abstemious.

"If I may suggest it, sir, cook has an excellent kidney pie on the way—"

"Cancel the sandwiches and flourish the pie. Right, Jonathan?" The Boss was stripping off his surplice and undoing his trousers.

"Right," I said. "And you can have first crack at the bath."

"Excuse me, sir," Parker interjected. "The other bath is already drawn. Just this way, sir." He indicated a second door and, opening it, revealed a second bathroom—a great big porcelain tub, fluffy towels on steam-heated racks, and an electric heater to warm the toes at.

There were clothes, too. When we had finished our baths, the Boss emerged in a black smoking jacket and flannels, and there were tweeds, a shirt, and underwear for me.

"You'll find some fairly stout boots over there." The Boss pointed. I tried them on, and they fitted me very well.

"Parker is good at this sort of thing," my father said. "Notice the beds."

I did. They were turned down, and from the bulge under the blankets, I detected the presence of pigs—those good stone hot-water bottles the Scots use to warm their sheets. (Modern metal pigs are rather a poor substitute.)

On a table by the fire, my father's drink was waiting, and in a minute, after a discreet knock, a table was wheeled in complete with what are called, I believe, "smoking viands." The viand I liked best was the kidney pie, from whose crust steam came pouring in a Christmas pattern. There were chips and scones and, of course, tea.

"It is time," said my father, "to explain this thing a little more thoroughly." (*High* time, *I* thought.) "The entire situation has changed and largely because of the delaying action in which you starred today. The people we are up against are the remnant of a drug-and-arms-running gang that I helped to destroy at the time of the Cuban revolution. On the side, they are professional agents, with loyalty only to money. Legitimate evidence of their illegitimate activities was in the possession of a —shall we say 'neutral'?—party who left the British Isles late this afternoon. I had only the space of today to get the papers from him. I knew where he was, and they didn't. They informed me last night that they had you in clutch and would trade you only for the papers. Regrettably enough from their point of view, they were unaware that their Edinburgh stronghold had been infiltrated."

"You mean Mrs. McGregor?"

He merely smiled. "Suffice it to say that because you kept out of their grasp through the day that is now ending—" he glanced at his watch and I at mine; it was five minutes to twelve—"because you kept out of their grasp, I had time and opportunity to possess myself of the evidence, get in touch with the Midlothian constabulary, and notify our embassy of what was going on."

"Which means—?"

"Which means, as I've said, that the whole situation is changed. In two ways. They who were the hunters are now the hunted. The cops are after 'em—or will be very soon. The papers I mentioned are being flown right now to the Home Office; names are named, addresses given. There will be an ingathering."

I helped myself to some more pie, and Parker entered.

"I beg your pardon, Mr. Five, but it occurred to me that a bottle of '59 Médoc might be acceptable." He polished two glasses, and my father said to me, "Go ahead. Take some. You've earned it.

"The thing is," he continued, "that the three lads who were at the school tonight may not be picked up. The police will want them, but I'll give you ten-to-one that they skedaddled with their wounded crony right after your battle. And whereas van Hoost wanted you today as a hostage—and wanted to prevent my securing the evidence —now that I have it, I'm afraid we—you and I—are no longer a means to an end. It is much more likely—if those gentlemen escape the law—that because of their spite and chagrin, we are out-and-out targets."

I smiled at him. "You're a pretty good dodger," I said.

He nodded. "I propose in this instance that we dodge together. Van Hoost may have had only an incidental interest in you until now, but—on his way to me—he is unlikely to forget the shot in Fang O'Reilly's leg."

"*Fang* O'Reilly? Oh, come now."

"That's his name. A former New York hood. From Chinatown. Very active for the On Leong Tong at one time."

"The tallest of the three?"

"That's the one. A rather unforgiving guy. From now on, if we have trouble, it will be aimed, not at our government or governmental interests, but at ourselves. I'm sorry that it's so, but it is." He paused. "Now wasn't there some talk of mountain climbing?"

The sheets on the comfortable bed were clean and cool, with a faint scent of lavender. The pig was warm. I went to sleep.

❖ 12 ❖

"They picked up one of them? Was he wounded? No?"

My father was speaking into the telephone. His voice had awakened me. It was bright morning.

"He talked? How much did he talk?"

The answer to this was a long series of croaks and clicks in which I could distinguish only a very few words.

My father was nodding, as if his correspondent could see over the wire. "You're probably right. No, send over something I haven't driven before, will you?" He looked at his watch. "About ten, I think. In the stable drive. Right. Right. Thanks very much. 'Bye."

He turned to me. "Ah, you're awake, are you? That's just as well, for I've ordered breakfast." As he spoke, there was a knock, and Parker entered with the rolling table. Juice, porridge, kippers, tea, and toast. Very welcome.

"That was the General, or Mr. Three as we call him," the Boss explained over the breakfast things. "One of last night's trio has been picked up. Regrettably, it's neither van Hoost *nor* O'Reilly. On the other hand, the bird they got didn't mind doing some singing. According to Mr. Three, he was nabbed for speeding in Leith, and his car turned out to have a phony registration—and blood on the floor."

"From the chap I shot?"

"I suppose so. The driver must have dropped his pals off somewhere along the line. He's a Glasgow knife-boy with a record as long as your arm, so they had no difficulty booking him. Said he'd been hired for the night by a Dr. Fisher to act as a bodyguard. Had no idea there'd be any trouble—but, confronted with the blood, he admitted that there had been. He identified the location of the school, where, he said, they were ambushed by machine-gun fire. He named O'Reilly as an American."

"Did he say where he dropped off Fang—I still can't believe that name—and his boss?"

"At the Portobello pool, apparently. Hm. At that hour it would have been closed, I'm afraid. Pity—if they wanted to swim." He speared a final wedge of kipper and washed it down with tea. "One other bit is rather interesting. This chap they nabbed seemed very much shaken up and implied that the doctor was off his head."

"Maybe he is. But what made the fellow think so?"

"Because on the ride back the doctor kept muttering about a bunch of flowers—or a couple of flowers, witness wasn't certain—and about how they had to be destroyed." He looked at me keenly across the table. "A couple of flowers—I wonder what or whom the doctor meant." He smiled.

I said, "I wonder."

For a moment or two the toast was hard to swallow.

"There's no doubt about it," said the Boss. "The Hollander is a vindictive man." (We took it for granted by now that van Hoost, Finch, and Fisher were one and the same.) "He is also a very clever one. I think you realize that luck played a considerable part in your successful adventure of yesterday. By the same token, you and I will both need luck—as well as brains—for as long as he remains at large. I have debated whether to try it together or to send you off to some sort of protective custody. On the whole, I think you are better with me. We are both better, I should say."

"I'm glad you feel that way"—and I was—"but do you seriously think he's going to be after us? I thought you said he was in trouble himself."

"Difficulties—yes. He is a marked man and wanted for extradition. He has indulged, however, in so many identities—and so successfully—that I'm not sure—even with the evidence that yesterday's breather enabled me to furnish—that the police are quite certain whom they're looking for. Interpol may have a slightly clearer picture."

"And meanwhile, we are the bait to draw him on?"

"Yes. That's about it. I hope you don't mind."

"Mind? I think it sounds terrific. What do we do—to lure him to his doom?"

"I think," said my father, "that all we have to do is travel about a bit with an eye out for the person or persons who seem to be taking the same trail. Actually, I'd thought we might as well go ahead with our climbing scheme."

I began, about then, to realize the strangeness of our position. In one sense, we wanted to evade the doctor's pursuit—at least that was *my* point of view. In another, we wanted to draw him on.

"I may say this," the Boss continued. "If we can keep

him chasing for a week, it is highly likely that enough additional information will have reached the authorities to make him really public property.

"We'll have to do a bit of to-and-fro. He will probably expect us to take some abnormal course. That's precisely why I favor following our former plan."

I could see what he meant. This was a guessing game in which routine might be more surprising than surprise —the expected course more startling than invention.

Breakfast over, the Boss lit his pipe and glanced at his watch.

"I asked them to bring around a car at ten. For reasons that will become clear, Parker is going along with us in the guise of chauffeur. He's out now buying you some walking gear. I expect your knapsack is still at Dr. Fisher's. Too bad I didn't pick it up with the milk."

As the Boss finished speaking, Parker knocked and entered. He was dressed in a neat gray driver's uniform.

"The car is ready, Mr. Five. I've stowed the gear in the boot." He conducted us to a side door, which gave onto a cobbled stable drive. The car was parked in a kind of architectural pocket. Behind it were the closed doors of the stable; house walls were on either side; high metal gates shut us off from the street.

And what a car! It was a bright blue convertible coupé —one of Maserati's new GT5000 Persias! I had only seen one other—and that was at Le Mans—but I knew the thing would do well over a hundred and fifty.

"Pleasantly conspicuous," said the Boss. "Well done, Parker."

"My hat!" I said feebly. "Is this creature ours?"

"Nothing is truly ours but life and love," the Boss

intoned. "No. Of course it isn't ours. It's a government wagon."

I had been aching to ask another vital question. "And the house—is it a government thingummy too?"

"It's a 'safe' house. Safe for our side, that is. Come along now, mount up."

He took his place behind the wheel and pointed me to the bucket seat beside him. Parker installed himself in the boot. My father flicked a gadget on the magnificent dashboard, and the driveway gates swung open. With a mighty purr we eased out onto the street, cornered, and were off with a roar. Pretty chic, I thought, with Parker sitting like a ramrod behind. Pretty chic, and—as the Boss had remarked—decidedly conspicuous.

I must say that Mr. Flower, Sr., can handle a motorcar. He told me once that he quit his amateur racing when my mother died; but I know that at one time he was urged to enter the Indy 500. He isn't reckless in the bad sense of the term, but he certainly makes time. And Scottish roads are a real test for anyone who wants to average as much as a mere forty.

We headed round the western end of the Forth and made the "Golden Lion" in Stirling for a late and lengthy luncheon. Without trying to be Temple Fielding, Jr., I should like to say that I think the "Golden Lion" puts on just about the best feed bag west of Aberfoyle. We ate in the private bar and polished off a pair of chops apiece. Parker wouldn't sit with us, although we asked him—he preferred, he said, to "remain in character" and was served accordingly in some secret purlieu sacred to retainers.

My father then proceeded to lay a trail. He had the porter telephone Gleneagles for reservations and indulged in a considerable chat about golf with one of the barmaids.

"Well, cheers then. We're off."

And off we were—eastward through Perthshire to the shores of Fife. But first the Boss made a telephone call of his own—from a roadside box some three miles out of Stirling.

"What was that about?" I asked him as he got back in the car.

"Simply to cancel our reservations at Gleneagles," he said. "We're going a bit farther. The more trails we lay, the busier our friends will be."

We wound up the day at St. Andrews, driving straight across Perthshire into the "kingdom" of Fife. From the hill above the town, the university buildings looked like ancient monuments, dark against the bright blue of the sea. My father signed us in at Blackwood's Hotel, and I looked over his shoulder at the register. "Jock Golding and Ewan Wilson," it read.

"Indeed?" I murmured. "Which am I?"

"You'd better be Golding—though I can think of few worse fates."

I knew from of old that my father's aliases were invariably the names of real people. "Who are they this time?" I asked.

"They were both college classmates of mine and should have no objection to lending their identity. Wilson is a rug dealer in South Philadelphia."

"And Golding?"

"Golding writes books with colored titles."

"Colored titles?"

"Yes—'The Blue Streak,' 'The Yellow Belly,' 'The Red Comyn,' and—let's see—'The Green Grocer' and 'The Black Watch.' There are others too."

I was bemused by my new identity.

"What about Parker?" I asked.

"Parker, at my request, has already gone on to the north. Our inconspicuous little vehicle will shortly be observed in the hills of Cupar Angus. We, in the meanwhile, will put in a day of golf. If not interrupted, that is. I trust you'll play better than your namesake."

We strolled over to the Royal and Ancient, which looks, I have always thought, like a relic of the mansion-building era in Pittsburgh's East End. The red-brown stone clubhouse is about as unlike our low spread-out country clubs in the States as a building could be. But then, it isn't a country club. It's the Royal and Ancient.

"No pseudonyms here," the Boss told me. "This is sanctuary."

Sure enough, he was greeted in proper style by the diminutive porter who admitted us.

"Come in, Major Flower. Come in, sir." (In Britain, one's military dignities are permanent.) "We didn't know you were in Scotland, sir. And this is Master Jonathan? My, my—he's a large lad now—and no doubt a bonny golfer, eh?"

My father and I had played the Old Course two years before when my golf had been anything but bonny. The Boss's own game is consistently good. He has what they call a grooved swing, and it doesn't seem to matter very much how infrequently he plays. I have noticed, however, that wherever his duties take him, a round or so is usually fitted in, and I know that he keeps clubs on tap at a dozen or more courses—from Troon to Tasmania.

We had tea under the painting of the former Prince of Wales, and Bobby Jones's portrait stared at us across the room. It was a bit late to think of playing, so we settled for a tour of the trophy cases and went back to Blackwood's with a quickened impression of the majesty and timelessness of golf.

My father made a curious comparison.

"It's like the Christian religion," he said of his favorite game. "That's probably why so many ministers play it. It calls for manners and morals. I have known a dozen or more crack golfers who have called strokes on themselves for merely touching a ball in address or for possibly—faintly possibly—grounding a club in a hazard. But manners and morals are a by-product of devotion. You have to accept the rules, and this"—he waved a hand that embraced the clubhouse—"this is where the rules are made. And then, beyond the rules there are far tougher requisites—a willingness to accept discipline. Yes—a reverence for tradition, ritual, the usage of many generations—of course. Vestments, almost. Plus fours had a sometime sanctity. But deeper down there is an absolute conviction that the game itself is good—good as the green of grass and the sturdy jargon of 'slice' and 'hook' and the cheerfulness of absolutely beaten hackers—the comradeship of the inept. That's golf, and I rather think that's Christianity, too."

It is not in the ordinary course of things that my father delivers a sermon. I forgave him, however, because this was over the dinner table, and he has a very Calvinistic background.

We ate well and slept soundly—except that in the middle of the night I roused myself just enough to ask him, "How far behind us are these guys? Do you honestly think they're after us?"

"After all the jigamaroo with the car and names and things?" His smile was a tolerant one. "It perhaps escaped your notice that at Wemyss the A.A. man was a fake?"

"You mean the little khaki guy who waved at us?"

"Precisely. If he'd been genuine, he would not have saluted. There was a speed trap just a mile farther on, and a real A.A. scout would have passed us without a sign—warning us by the omission. I have a feeling that we'll see that scout again."

We went to sleep.

13

Nine-thirty the next morning found us on the first tee of
the Old Course, from which point of vantage I promptly
drove my ball into the burn that wanders across the fair-
way. My caddie, a rather talkative youngster of sixty-five or
so, produced a long-handled net from under some whins
and fished the ball out of the roiling water.

"Ye'll no do that again," said he. Whereupon I dropped
the ball behind me, looked up to see where my hit was flying, and dumped the thing back in the burn.

"Ech," said the caddie. "Likes it was because ye didna'
play a second from the tee." I dropped again. "Change
your club, then," he insisted. "Try a wee four-wood. Yon's
as good a baffie as there is."

I took what he offered, relaxed a bit, and hit out straight
and true. I was glad to be home in eight. After that things
got better. I made only two bunkers—one a yawning gulf
of sand that I had to play out of backward. The enormous
double greens were a problem through the first nine, but
coming home I had begun to get the feel of my putter.

I can't say that the caddie helped me much. His estimate
of distances was only fair, and as I've said, he was surprisingly full of conversation for a dour Scot, asking me all sorts

of questions—about where I'd played before and how long we were staying in St. Andrews and where we were going next on our holiday. To the last question I could truthfully say that I hadn't the least idea, a casual attitude that he seemed to find unworthy.

"Ye've a motor, I take it?" (I shall not attempt a full transliteration of his burr.)

I baffled him still further with my answer. "In a way we do."

He gave me a long look, and I experienced one of those spasmodic resentments that people my age have to get used to. He wouldn't dream of talking to my father the way he talked to me. And the conviction grew in me that certain folk use children—youngsters, adolescents, what you will—as saps and tunnels for the undermining of their elders.

At the eighteenth tee the Boss needed a four for an eighty. He had me dormy—I was still enduring the effects of hole number one. We both drove well, but he hooked his second into a trap. My own brassie was straight but short. His wedge shot landed twenty inches from the pin. My pitch was twenty feet past. I ran the putt a yard—or perhaps forty inches—to the right of the hole. I missed. He sank. Two down. Period.

Over lunch at the R. and A., we discussed our game—and, incidentally, the caddies.

"That character of mine," I said, "was the most talkative Scot—"

"Along what lines?" My father was smiling at me again, an irritatingly compassionate expression—sympathy for a cretin, more or less.

"Oh, he wanted to know where we came from and

whether we had a car and where we were heading—that sort of thing."

"A rather curious bag-toter. You might be interested in knowing that *my* caddie never laid eyes on yours before today. My man told me that yours kept asking him questions about distance and direction—as if it were his first tour of the course."

"Then that explains his uncertainty in recommending clubs."

"It explains more than that, I'm afraid. Had you no idea that you were being pumped—intentionally?"

A glimmer of light dawned. "You mean he was one of the—?"

"One of the opposition? It could be. Too large a number of people have been connected with that outfit—in petty capacities and incidental rôles—for all to be rounded up. As long as they get their pay, their's not to reason why."

As we walked back to the hotel to get our packs, an A.A. scout drove his motorcycle slowly up the High Street.

"Aha, the mobile unit," my father said. "I'm surprised —and rather disappointed—that he isn't after Parker."

The Firth of Tay was capped with suds that afternoon, and the ferry rolled like a rocking chair. Over in Dundee the sun shone on the marmalade factories, and beside us a train crept timidly over the long, low railroad bridge.

"There go the clubs," said my father, gesturing vaguely toward the bridge.

"What clubs?" I asked.

"The golf clubs. I had them checked to Carnoustie. We're in for another day of golf—if the weather holds."

We hiked to the station, had some tea, and caught one of those two-car diesels that answer the passenger problem in most of Scotland. The golf clubs we had used in the morning were stacked in that portion of the forward car that served as a guard's van. Twenty minutes later we were skirting miles of seashore golf course, parallel to the railroad. The sea was a blue-gray, and the concrete defense installations—a relic of the forties—looked like outsize barges on the rocks.

"Take us, please, to Mrs. Morton's house," my father told the driver of the taxi. "On the Lang Way."

"Yes, sir. Very good, sir. Here for a bit of golf?" He was a pink-cheeked boy about a year older than myself.

"We are indeed. But perhaps not for long."

What I am writing is not intended to be a travelogue. Each reader must taste the joys of Scotland for himself. I can't help mentioning, however, the stony neatness of Carnoustie—the crisp curbs and tiny gardens.

Mrs. Morton's house was larger than most with a six-foot wall and a six-foot hostess. She had apparently known the Boss for years, and obviously she expected us.

"Come away in, Major. And you too, Posy. That's what they call you, isn't it?"

I said, "Yes ma'am." And the three of us proceeded to take apart a noble tea.

"By the way," said Mrs. Morton, "there was an A.A. man who called this afternoon. Something about your car. Have you a car, Major? He said there'd been a complaint or a request for service or something of the sort. Described some great exotic motor."

The Boss was obviously intrigued. "Was this a local chap?" he asked. "Someone in the neighborhood, I mean?"

"I'd never seen him before in my life."

"What did you tell him then?"

"That I'd never even heard of you. And by the way," said Mrs. Morton, "who are you this trip, anyway?"

"We left St. Andrews as Golding and Wilson, a pair of itinerant golfers—at least as far as the hotel people were concerned. The R. and A. knew us, of course. But they don't know us here—at least not at the golf course. So we might as well use our aliases. Or maybe even a new pair." He paused. "I wonder how they learned about this house."

"You're referring to the A.A. laddie?" My father nodded. "Too many of you have been here too often."

"I should be sorry to think that. You've been far too helpful for us to be able to get along without you."

I gathered that here again was a "safe" house and wondered how many of them were scattered over Britain and the Continent.

We were shown to separate rooms with a bath between them. Early to bed, we slept well and long, enjoyed a generous breakfast in the late morning, and made our way by taxi to the middle clubhouse, where we signed in as Golding and Wilson and asked for caddies. The woman at the desk was most apologetic; there were no caddies available —if we had phoned ahead, in the middle of the week, we would understand—et cetera.

"The trouble is," my father explained, "we've neither of us ever played Carnoustie. I'm afraid we'll have a bit of difficulty finding our way."

"It's mostly out and back," said the woman. "And I can gie' ye cairts, of course."

The Boss and I are not very keen on "cairts," but there seemed no alternative until a young man with a tankard in his hand—who had been studying the trophies of the late MacDonald Smith—offered to help us out. He was the only other occupant of the lounge.

"If ye'll take the carts, gentlemen, I'll be glad to guide you round." He had very white teeth in a very brown face.

"This is Eric Lindsay," our hostess told us. "He's a course ranger—ye'll understand he keeps people moving along—and the likes of that."

"Traffic's light the day," said the ranger.

We took him up on his offer and were glad we had. He knew the course like the proverbial palm of his hand and was far better than the average caddie at advice on clubs.

Our round was ordinary enough—except for two items: the wind and the wanderer.

The wind was absolutely phenomenal. Nowhere—nowhere from Eastward Ho to Pebble Beach—have I ever seen its match. We had to hang onto the caddie carts or they would have sailed away from us along the fairways. I hit a five-iron as well as I ever hit a five-iron in my life; the ball went out and up—then drifted back at me like a homing pigeon. Of course, when the gale was behind you, you bashed the thing a mile; but for fully half the match we were beating our shots into the teeth of a breeze that laid the sea grass flat and made helpless airborne monkeys of the gulls.

Eric didn't actually caddie for us, but he was very helpful in holding down our "cairts." On the twelfth hole—I think it was—he was restraining the Boss's bag (which showed every sign of taking off for Norway) when I saw him draw out the most likely next club—a three-wood—and hold it ready to deliver.

Everybody knows what a "double take" is—where the

comic victim sees something happen, but it doesn't register, and he turns away unaware, and then it hits him and he snaps back horrified. Well, Eric did a double take at my father's wood. Then, very calmly, with no word of explanation, he put his fingers in his mouth and blew a long, sad whistle. It was exceptionally high in pitch and well calculated to carry against the wind. It reminded me of the kind of signal that Scottish shepherds use to command their dogs—except that it was more sustained.

At the moment I was fifty yards behind. I saw my father look up and then pivot, scanning the shore.

"What on earth was that for, Eric?" I asked the question as soon as I caught up with him. By then, he was jotting down a score—probably my six on the preceding hole.

"What, sir? Oh, the whistle, sir. Sorry about that. But there are petries out there by the dunes. Very scarce, you know."

"Petries?"

"Yes, sir. Birds. Gulls, almost, but with a smaller body and a sort of lapstreak marking. Clinker-built, you might say."

I had not expected that the course ranger would turn out to be an ornithologist, but you never know. Especially in Britain, where the hardest-boiled retired colonel writes lyrics in his garden and publishes books on the cultivation of the orchis.

We played on.

And then I saw the wanderer—a solitary figure in the distance. One could determine that he was dressed in tweeds—a cap and plus fours, apparently—but at three hundred yards, it was impossible to see his face.

"There'll be one I should speak to"—so Eric informed

me; and he took off at a sprinter's pace toward the stranger. So far as I could see, they exchanged no conversation, and our guide was back with us almost at once. Nothing else happened, except that with a kind of shy persistency the wanderer kept with us—out of shouting range, particularly in that wind—but moving as we moved and watching our shots with a concentration they hardly deserved.

At the seventeenth, he disappeared. We wound up all even, and my father gave Eric a tip, which was at first refused and then, reluctantly, accepted. At the clubhouse there was no sign of the wanderer. Very politely, Eric offered to call us a taxi. He seemed a little surprised that we hadn't our own car.

"Just for fun," said the Boss, "may I have our card? I think it's an eighty-six for me—and an eighty-four for Jock, isn't it?"

"Jock," I thought. "Oh, yes: 'Jock Golding'—not too big a switch from Jonathan."

Eric poked at various pockets. "I'm dreadfully sorry, sir. I must have dropped the card along the way." He looked at us apologetically. "I could easily fill out another —and you're quite right about the scores."

"O.K.," my father said. "Write one out, and we'll put it in our scrapbooks."

The taxi came, and we sat in the back seat, each with a golf bag between his knees.

"You realize that he gave a note to the watcher?" My father sounded more intrigued than concerned.

"Who—our ranger?"

"None other. What did you think had happened to our scorecard?"

I remembered Eric's busy writing just after the wanderer appeared. The pursuit, I gathered, had not slackened. My father was laughing quietly to himself.

"I did it," he confessed. "I did it."

"Did what?"

"I'll tell you after dinner."

And after dinner he told me. Or rather he showed me —with his driver. He was positively rueful.

"Old age has got me," he said. "I've done a lot of stupid things over the years, but this takes the cake." I had no idea what he was talking about. "We sign in at the club," he went on, "as Golding and Wilson. And look—" He handed me the one-wood, his thumb pointing to a thin white band below the grip. In tidy lettering, the label read: "Major Oregon Flower."

The Boss is not particularly happy about his Christian name. If the clubs had been banded at St. Andrews, however, no mitigation was possible.

"Off for other climes tomorrow," he said. "Meanwhile, a good night's sleep."

Unfortunately, I had no reply, and we settled down to maximum slumber—up to the point when I woke up and saw a human being standing by my window.

I say a human being because he looked like one—but vaguely.

✤ 14 ✤

There were no lights on, and I had only the moon and a shape to guide me. The shape came closer to my bed. It was one of those horrible things that you dream—when you're very young—and then people say to you that it's all a nasty nightmare and you mustn't worry, dear.

I'm sure the bed must have been shaking. Certainly *I* was. Then I heard my father's voice, speaking very softly.

"It's just me, but keep your voice down. There's somebody outside. I heard him getting over the wall, and he's in the garden now."

"Why don't we shout and watch him run?"

"No. I want him to break and enter. It'll be one more charge against him. I'm going downstairs to constitute a welcoming committee. You stay up here."

"But—" It occurred to me that the intruder might not be alone.

"No buts. That's an order. I'll call you if I need any help. Listen!" There was the faint sound of metal on metal, just below my window. For a moment my father's shadow remained visible, head cocked. Then it disappeared into the bathroom that led to his quarters.

Total silence followed. In blackness almost palpable, I

crept to the window and looked out. It was too dark to see anything. I tiptoed back and sat on the bed and listened.

To nothing. Then, to a soft scraping sound from outside. A window going up? I went to the door that gave on the corridor, opened it about six inches, and listened.

To nothing. Then, downstairs, the snick of a door latch.

I usually obey the Boss's orders pretty precisely. But after all, he hadn't said—in so many words—that I was to stay in the bedroom.

I pussyfooted it to the banister and looked down. At nothing. Then the guarded gleam of an electric torch skipped along the downstairs wainscoting.

Without any warning there was a tremendous crash. Instantly, all the lower lights were burning. I nipped down the stairs and nearly scragged my father who, it seemed, had been in ambush on the landing.

"Come along," he said. "This way—to the kitchen!"

We scooted through the hall, now brightly lighted, crossed the dining room, and shouldered open the door to the pantry.

A memorable sight met our eyes.

Stretched out on the floor, in an attitude of complete and compulsive indifference, was a long, thin stranger. In his left hand—or just out of it—was a flashlight, the bulb still pathetically alive. An oriental look about his very yellow face hinted at his origin.

Over this victim of the night's activities stood Mrs. Morton, all six feet of her swathed in a flannel nightie, reminiscent of the deathbed of Voltaire. In her hand was an iron poker. She spoke apologetically.

"You gentlemen need not have fashed yourselves. I'm sorry for your disturbance."

My father simply stood there, his hands on his hips, relishing the scene in all its Gothic beauty. At length he drew a long breath, and "Wonderful!" he said. "Congratulations, Mrs. Morton. You seem to have fair copped him one. Isn't that the expression?"

"I believe so, Major. And if you're totting up the score, I'd like to call attention to the fact that he was armed." The recumbent one's jacket had fallen open, and a loaded shoulder holster was plainly to be seen.

The Boss poked him gently with a slippered toe. "As on a mission sent," he said. "This will require a little thought."

"And tea, I think," said Mrs. Morton.

My father nodded. "Oh yes, tea by all means."

He stooped and removed the sleeper's pistol.

"The cops?" asked Mrs. Morton. "Or something else?" She was putting the kettle on.

"I'm not sure," my father said, and looked again at the figure on the floor. "It's Fang all right, and we truly have him with the goods. But I'm not sure. Just let me weigh the possibilities. Our friend won't have much to say for another hour or so."

We went upstairs, and it was only then that I noticed that, with the exception of shoes and socks, my father was fully dressed.

"I knew they'd come tonight," he said, "after that business on the golf course. And honestly, I'm not sure. If we call the cops, it means assurance of our identity, all sorts of questions, delay, and legal process."

"Can't Mrs. Morton simply report him as a burglar?"

"She'd have to make a statement as to the occupants of the house, their part in the fracas, and all that. No," he said, as I inserted myself into trousers. "No. I think I have a better idea. It will, to be sure, involve a couple of phone calls."

We went back downstairs as the first ray of dawn started to light the sky. I settled to my tea—plus ham and eggs—and listened to my father on the telephone in the corridor. Mr. Fang O'Reilly was still snoozing on the kitchen floor, but his hostess had considerately placed a pillow under his head.

"Five, here," my father said. "All serene, thank you. Just a bit of a disposal problem. What? Good idea. How long will it take you? An hour to get here? Right. We'll have him ready for you. Oh yes, we'll pack his pockets with the stuff. And by the way, Parker, use your Macnicol identification, will you—the one with the altered date. Right. 'Bye."

If Parker had ever driven for Alec Macnicol's father, it was news to me. But now my father was making a cross-country call to a Wester Ross exchange. There was a long wait and obvious symptoms of remoteness. Finally, "Hello? Hello? Is that Menzies? No? I'm dreadfully sorry to be calling so early. May I ask to whom I'm speaking—this is Major Flower. Oh, young Grant? Yes, yes, right—we met the day school closed. I understand; there's just the one phone. And you were downstairs for a bite. Quite. But look here, could you possibly put me on to your host? I know it's inconvenient. But I think if you tell him—oh, he's there? Thanks awfully."

A pause. Then, "Macnicol—Oregon Flower here. Yes. Sorry to bother you, but I thought you ought to know that my man Parker is using your credentials in a bit of business that will probably wind up at Stonehaven. What's that? Good man, I thought you wouldn't. The thing is,

113

though, that I don't want him held for prolonged questioning, and if he can say you need him right away—and they can substantiate by phone—all's well. *Compris?* Splendid. Thanks so much. Incidentally, give my best to the Lord Lieutenant. I may be up in his territory before long. Right. Right. I hope so, 'Bye.''

A sound from the kitchen suggested that our Sino-Irish friend was coming back to awareness. We found Mrs. Morton, now fully clad, leaning over him like an angler over a new-hooked bass—or rather, pike: he had the build and jaw of a Great Northern. He was acting, however, rather like a sand dab. After one or two tentative flops, he relaxed on his pillow and went back to dreamland.

"Good," said my father, "now we can resume work on him."

He went swiftly through O'Reilly's clothing. Having removed the clip from the small automatic, he rather surprisingly put the gun back in the shoulder-holster. From an inside jacket pocket he removed a passport (U. S., green) and from the trousers some British currency, thirty-odd pounds and a few shillings. My father handed the money to Mrs. Morton.

"For the pot," he said. "Besides, you bent the poker."

Then from his own pocket he took a wad of notes and put them in O'Reilly's clothing where the latter had kept his own cash. The Boss stood up, dusting off his hands in a gesture of accomplishment. "That, as we say at home, ought to fix his little red wagon—and save us a good bit of time and trouble." He surveyed the sleeper once more. "No wallet, no mail, no papers. I'd search his shoesoles if I didn't think he was too unimportant to be trusted with a code key."

We heard a car outside.

"Run and let Parker in," the Boss said. "We mustn't make him climb the wall."

I opened the garden gate, and our redoubtable Jehu of two days before gave me a smart salute.

"Delighted to hear from you, sir. I trust I haven't kept anyone waiting?"

"Not a bit," I assured him. "This way, Parker—to the kitchen. We're keeping your—er, errand—your package, that is, on the floor."

His reply astonished me, for it's always rather shocking when the punctilious turns out to be macabre.

"Not a cold-storage job, I hope?"

"No," I said. "Not quite."

In the kitchen, good mornings and brief introductions were exchanged.

Mrs. Morton insisted that she had "met Mr. Parker before under other circumstances." I didn't doubt it a bit.

"This," said my father, waving a foot at the downfallen, "is a sorry incidence of *hubris* and the fatal flaw. The fellow underestimated Scottish heroines. Never read about Margaret Barlass. Pity. Give him a 22-90, Parker, and then join us in the sitting room for a briefing."

"Right, sir." Parker was extracting from the pocket of his uniform a black leather case that reminded me of Dr. Fisher. It looked medical.

"A 22-90, you said, sir?"

"Right. Look him over for a bit. Then we'll make the pattern."

From the black case Parker drew a tool that was certainly a fancy hypodermic. (Remarkable, the way my father's friends and acquaintances consider a needle standard equipment.) A few minutes later he joined us in front of the fire for tea and Forfar bridies.

"Patient well along, sir," he told my father. "I took the liberty of checking his skull. Perhaps it would not be offensive to inform Mrs. Morton that she narrowly missed the *medulla oblongata*. A very vulnerable spot, you know. However"—he sighed happily—"it appears that no real cranial damage has been incurred—"

"Parker," the Boss broke in, "you talk like an undertaker."

"Thank you, sir," said Parker. "My father was engaged in the profession, and I rejoice that I have not escaped its idiom."

"I rejoice with you, Parker—you recall the passage: 'Rejoice with them that do rejoice and weep with them that weep.' Seems to fit the situation nicely . . .

"Now as to further details. You, Parker, are to cart our bundle"—he pointed to the kitchen—"to any police station in the neighborhood of Stonehaven. You are, you will wish to remember, chauffeur to Lord Inchdarroch, otherwise known as the Macnicol. He sent you last night on an errand—not to be too precise, let us say in Aberdeen.

"On the way south (for further shopping or something of the sort), you nearly ran over a man, lying unconscious by the roadside. Subsequent to your gentle ministrations, he returned to partial consciousness but was unable to give you any information as to his identity and circumstance. Despite your obligation to return as promptly as possible to your employer, considerations of humanity prompted you to reach the police and ensure the safety of your passenger.

"You will insist that you are in a hurry to get off. Throw

Lord Inchdarroch's name about in a vulgar way and, if necessary, suggest that they check with him by phone—"

"My urgency has been intimated to his lordship?" For Parker, this was a major interruption.

"It has. You will have prompt substantiation. I've talked to him myself."

"One more question, sir. Is there some method by which I can—er—unite my passenger with the police in a more permanent way?"

"I was coming to that. They *may* recognize him. The metropolitan police almost certainly would. County constabulary—I don't know. Your story to him when he wakes up should be the same as your story to them—finding him by the roadside and doing the good Samaritan. He will have no way of checking its truth, and I rather imagine he won't be very clear as to events immediately preceding. When the cops ask him how he got hurt, he'll either have to invent some cock-and-bull story or tell them he's lost his memory. He's hardly likely to inform them that when last conscious he was engaged in armed felonious entry."

"Suppose he wakes up on the way," I put in, "and refuses to go with you to a police station? Do you knock him out again or what?"

Parker smiled. "I hardly think that will be necessary, sir. When he awakes, I shall inform him that we are on our way to a doctor—because of the lump on his head and probable internal injuries—"

"Internal injuries?"

"*Probable* internal injuries. No phrase terrifies them more, sir. Besides, that kind always like to make for a town. The countryside alarms them. It is, so to speak, too clean."

"A nice analysis, Parker; and you might add," said my father, "that anyone who's had a good dose of 22-90 remains docile for some time—if not positively groggy." Turning again to Parker, he went on. "You are probably not unacquainted with the art of extracting a tip?"

"I accept a *pourboire* from time to time, sir."

"Well, even at a cost to dignity, I want you to get one out of this bird—the earlier on, the better—and then, if the police appear to have no suspicion of him as other than an unfortunate victim of an accident, you are to take your note (he has nothing smaller to give you) and ask the desk sergeant to give you his expert opinion of it. A search of our friend should certainly ensue, and I rather think that some grounds will be found for his detention."

Parker's eyebrows went up in pawky approbation. "May I ask, sir, whether he habitually—er—shoves the queer?"

"Actually, no. Between ourselves, this is an isolated instance."

"An *affaire arrangée?*" (Parker was obviously pleased with that one.)

"I fear so. The stuff is very poor and therefore easily identified for what it is. I have used it before in similar situations."

"Very good, sir. And now if there's nothing further, perhaps I might have a hand with my charge."

We helped him bundle Mr. Fang O'Reilly into the car. It was not the Maserati Persia but a big black Bentley. I was amazed to see on the door a familiar crest and Alec's father's motto: "Give him an Inch."

❖ 15 ❖

It was the deliberate attempt to run us down near Pitlochry that determined my father's next move.

"I was beginning to think that they might be discouraged, but apparently not."

Toward the end of a day's hike, we were walking the rather narrow road that leads to town from the east. As usual, we faced such oncoming traffic as there was. Pleasantly tired, our reflexes were probably less quick than usual. As we neared a blind turn, a big green lorry swept into sight. It was sixty or seventy yards away and traveling much too fast. Instinctively, we swung to the roadside at our right, but my father didn't stop with that. In a flash, he was over the low stone wall, pulling me over with him in a somersault of flying knapsacks.

The lorry didn't miss the wall by more than two inches. With a snarl it shot by in a trail of diesel smoke.

We lay on the ground, both panting. Finally, the Boss got up and began to brush himself off.

"That," he said, "was too stupid to be unintentional," and he expressed his regret at the dedicated villainy of certain people. . . .

It was, as I have said, this brush with the untimely that fixed my father's next decision. We ought now, he felt, to hole up—not, according to his earlier thought, in such hideaways as "safe" houses, but out of sight, among friends if possible, and, in case the pursuit continued, in a position where we could defend ourselves. One such place seemed obvious.

You can't go to provincial police and make the announcement—"Somebody tried to run me down with a truck." Particularly not when you were too scared to get the license or see the driver or observe any markings.

We caught the bus for Inverness. The North Road was busy, but the farther we went, the less busy it became. We carried no more than half a load of passengers—including a number of tweedy nabobs whose long leather cases and roseate complexions proclaimed them fishermen. By contrast, two or three others of the company, though equipped with the tubes and sacks that are a necessary preface to salmon, looked anything but rugged. I noticed that my father kept an eye on these latter; nor did he look particularly pleased when they descended at our destination. We saw them again in the lobby of the station hotel. The next morning one of them was outside the hire-service office where we rented a Zephyr.

And on our way farther north we were twice passed by cars that seemed to be determined to keep in our neighborhood and were manned by pasty-faced sportsmen.

Inchdarroch is very nearly the back of beyond. Miles past Achnasheen and the brow of Ben Dearg, it is far from the nearest railroad and is chiefly served by a ribbon of black-top trail, the ups and downs of which—with lay-bys every half a mile—appear too narrow for a baby Austin but are somehow navigated by Jaguars and Daimlers.

The countryside is typical of the West Highlands—ranks of craggy mountains, largely treeless; breath-taking vistas, first of black lochs and blue, then of the sea; and all under a sky whose constant change casts deep cloud shadows racing down the glens or opens golden patches on the slopes. We were early for the heather, though here and there the gray side of a crag showed faintly purple. All about us, if we cut the engine and listened, there was the sound of water—not the drip and splash of the American northwoods, but the hushed fall of a thousand burns boiling their way to the sea. Now and then, a curlew called, and once we heard an eagle scream somewhere out of sight. Otherwise—silence, the silence of an unwearied, ageless land.

Until, as we stopped the Zephyr on a hill crest and drew in air that my father said tasted like whisky (Talisker! he called it), we heard from our right the one sound that is unforgettable for Scotsmen or for anyone else—the skirling of a pipe across the hills.

As we listened, the music died a dark chromatic death. I looked by chance to our left—away from the pipe sound —at a hilltop half a mile or so away. Near its top stood a solitary figure, scanning the horizon. For just an instant the lowering sun glinted on what might have been binoculars.

To reach the castle of Inchdarroch, you drive first to the village of Balloch Inch, a straggling street of small white houses built close together and facing the sea loch that is known as "Acair Padraich" or Padraich's Harbor. From here, it is claimed, St. Patrick sailed on one of his voyages.

There is a post office, a police station, a church, and an inn called "The Twelve Inches." We saw no sign of a school.

Drifting down our sea-view hill, we drove the length of the clachan and followed the coast as it curved its arm to embrace the loch. It was nearly sunset, and the castle in the distance seemed far out from land, its towers sharp and sun-stained against a yellow sky. From the hills on our left, wisps of smoke betrayed the hidden crofts of shepherds and ghillies. My father explained that while Lord Inchdarroch's land extended up the shore and inward from the village, these crofts and mountains belonged to Sir Agravaine McVittie.

It was four miles from the village to the causeway giving access to the castle. Although the stonework from road to island had obviously been improved and worked on through the centuries, the central portion of the bridge was much too narrow for a car, and that anything wider than a horse had ever crossed the moat, I thought unlikely. It was certain that Parker's Bentley would never have made it.

As far as our driving was concerned, this was a dead end. We left the Zephyr at one side and advanced upon the causeway. The yellow of the western sky was tipped with scarlet banners.

We were unexpected guests. My father had discussed the propriety of a phone call but had decided against it.

"I don't see how a pay box could do any harm," I had said as we drove through Lochluichart in the afternoon.

"It's not the pay-box end I'm worried about. Don't you remember what happened at Plummet Lodge?"

"Not what you mean, I'm afraid."

"Well how do you suppose they knew that you were headed for the consulate?"

"You—you're telling me that your call to Lady Hamilton was tapped?"

"Not tapped, necessarily. Listened in on, more likely. It's simpler, and I happen to know that Sophia has two or three extensions."

"Then someone in the household—?"

"I've had my eye on the butler for several years. Therefore, the mistake was wholly mine. But I don't believe we'll run the same risk with Inchdarroch. Faithful retainers I'm sure they have, but what is that cheery old New England saying? 'There's a rotten apple in every barrel,'—that's it."

At the head of the causeway, a cobbled forecourt led up to the ancient gate. Once across the water, one went to the left and mounted steps with two-foot risers to a great oak door, where, most suprisingly, there was a doorbell. A pull, of course, but even such amenities are unexpected in a stony fortress built five centuries ago. At the rear of the courtyard, a brawny creature in a kilt was cleaning a mess of rabbits. He looked up at our arrival but did not speak.

"Good evening," said my father. "Is Lord Inchdarroch at home?"

"Ay, he iss," and he went back to his eviscerating.

Unexpectedly, before we had time to ring, the door opened. Standing on the threshold was Mary Pigtail Hamilton.

"Why, Posy! And Major Flower! What in the world are you doing up here? We thought you were in Paris."

"Indeed? That was an interesting notion. May we come in?"

"Who is it, Mary?" A deep voice boomed from the stony background. In a moment we were being greeted by a small and wiry Scot, red of hair and beard. With a greater presence and another coloring, he might have passed for the renowned Commander Whitehead. He wore the kilt, and his hands, which I realized were prosthetic, were covered by black leather gloves.

"Welcome to Inchdarroch," said the laird. "I'm delighted to see you, Major. And you, young Flower. Alec'll be very pleased. He's out on the water just now—with your schoolmate Grant."

Reunion All Around, I thought—as in Ronald Knox.

"We really must apologize for not advising you of our coming," the Boss said.

"Not at all. We simply feared, after yesterday's message, that we shouldn't see you this year."

"Yesterday's message?"

"Ay. Your friend—what's his name?—the chap who's fishing McVittie's water—Finch, that's it—took the trouble to walk over from 'The Twelve Inches' to let me know."

I looked at my father and he looked at me.

"To let you know—what?"

"Why, that you had been called away to Paris. I thought it jolly decent of him. Told me he's a Queen's Messenger. Romantic life, I should think—though he isn't quite the type I'd always pictured."

"No," said my father. "No, not quite."

"He was much intrigued by the castle," said Mary.

"Oh?" The Boss's voice was quietly inquisitive. "How much of it did he see?"

Lord Inchdarroch laughed. "We gave him the usual

treatment, I'm afraid—without the two-bob fee. From the dungeon to the fiery tower."

"It sounds to me," said my father—and then said nothing more.

Except that in his bedroom, he finished his sentence. "It sounds to me," he said, "as if he really cased the joint."

❖ 16 ❖

I slept late the next morning and barely returned to the
land of the living when Mary Pigtail threw a hunting boot
at my bed. Still in my p.j.'s, I chased her down a spiral
staircase to a door with "MCCCCLVII" carved over it.

Most Americans, I suspect, would prefer a cozy living
room with baseboard heat to a baronial hall with an open
fire. Nor would many of my friends in Wynnewood sleep
with comfort in a springless four-poster surrounded by
flagstone flooring.

But I liked it. When Mary's boot hit me in the ribs and
I managed to open my eyes, there was a coal fire ready-lit,
tea under a cozy at my elbow, and a great big tub of hot
water that must have taken somebody several trips of cop-
per cans to fill.

Alec and Tommy had gone fishing again that morning,
and Mary Pigtail—with a total disregard of them—took
me through things from top to bottom—or rather from
bottom to top. The dungeon, now used as a wine cellar,
had fifteenth-century gyves hanging from its walls. The
narrow spiral stairways were punctuated by sconces, ready
for *flambeaux*. The big room, which for some reason they
call the "Pit," was two stories high with an enormous fire-

place at one end and a gallery at the other. There were no actual suits of armor, but there were claymores and targes on the walls, interspersed with portraits of long-dead Macnicols. One painting—it was of the laird's grandfather —was an obvious Sargent; two others were Romneys, and oddly enough, there was a Gilbert Stuart portrait of Washington.

Mary Pigtail took me—via another spiral staircase—to what I suppose would be called the battlements. There was a surprising quantity of flat. (I mean, I had always thought that castles had either slanted top floors or none at all.) But Inchdarroch was an exception to the rule. The roof was broad and walkable, and Mary led me onto what they called the "Fiery Tower"—which was not a tower, actually, but a great bundle of iron braces, crisscrossed and ready to contain the burning of a body or a bucket.

"That," she said, "is the communications center of Inchdarroch."

I wasn't certain of what she meant. "How?" I asked.

"If you'll drop the Indian dialect—"

"No—I mean—how does the beacon basket operate as a communications center? And how do you know about it?"

She explained to me that the ancient custom, if the castle were attacked, was to call the clansmen in by a series of fires lighted in the beacon. The peculiar situation of Inchdarroch with regard to its tenants and levies—the fact that they must necessarily come from some miles away because of the oddly distributed lairdship—heightened the importance of a signal and made its long-range visibility essential.

I am not, as a rule, a good tourist. Museums weary me, and I develop a kind of claustrophobia when a palace guide closes a door behind my group and begins his pitch with "Please keep moving in this direction only"—pretty much the point of no return. I had none of these symptoms, however, as I wandered about with Mary.

It struck me that with the exception of the "Pit," all of the rooms were small. Mary reminded me that the smaller, the warmer. "Besides," she said, "with eight feet of stone between you and the open air, you've used up most of your space in fortification. A bedroom like yours, only twelve feet square, actually takes up more than seven hundred square feet."

I did some mental arithmetic. She was pretty close. (Try it for yourself.)

Everybody was on deck for lunch. Alec and Tom had killed a gorgeous salmon. (I should say "fish," for in the Highlands all "fish" are salmon, and you stoop to name only the lesser breeds.) There were hot buttered scones and a winey rabbit stew. I was mopping up my remnants of the latter when things began to happen. I mean to say that from stew time onward a series of events built up toward climax.

The man who was serving us left the room and came back a moment later with a look of concern.

"Begging your pardon, sir—it iss Gavin Dhu."

Lord Inchdarroch frowned. "What's he want?" The red beard wagged whenever he spoke, a separate action for each change of mood. "We're in the midst of lunch. Fetch him in, will you?"

A big ghillie in gamekeeper's clothing, Gavin Dhu had a Macnicol look about him but was black of hair and blue of cheek. It was he we had seen in the courtyard.

"What is it, Gavin Dhu?" The conversation surely would

have been in Gaelic but for the presence of us Sassenachs.

"It iss a thing you should know, sir." (The accent of the Western Highlander is almost Teutonic in its gutturals and hissings.) "Upon McVittie's approaches there are today strange guns—at least seven—I haf counted them, but there may be more. No one iss beating for them, and they shoot nothing. They are strangers and uncertain of the hills; but they have glasses, two or three, and they watch."

"Probably a bird club," said Lord Inchdarroch.

"I think not, laird. Pird clubs do not carry rifles."

"Rifles! Are you sure?" The question was an affront, and Gavin did not deign to answer.

The laird looked across at my father. "Do you suppose, Major—that is to say, is there any chance that—?"

"Some chance, at least," said the Boss. "But wouldn't McVittie know?"

"He's a way off, I'm sorry to say. Too much drink taken —at all hours. And Rory—Rory MacLeod—that's his head gamekeeper—what about Rory, Gavin Dhu?"

"He iss not on McVittie's land, sir. He iss at London or some such—for why, only the Father knows." He crossed himself, and I realized that Inchdarroch was one of those enduring enclaves of the Roman faith that have survived both swords and centuries.

"I say," Alec broke in. "Do you suppose Sir Agravaine's being invaded?"

"There is such a thing as organized poaching," his father told him. "But if they're not shooting at all—

"We can hardly send Gavin over to investigate. There's still a bit of bad blood between our people, you know. Silly but a fact. In ancient times the two families were fast friends."

129

"*I* know," said Alec. "*We'll* stalk 'em. Tommy and Posy and I. What? May we? Do say we may! You're a stalker, aren't you, Posy?"

"I've only gone once after stag," I said, remembering the occasion vividly. "The gralloch made me sick."

"He was only eleven," my father put in. "You know, Macnicol," he went on, "I think the boys may have a pretty good idea. Let *them* track over there for a bit. They've no right to, of course; but considering the circumstances, it's probably for McVittie's good. The deep concern of friendly neighbors—that sort of thing. What do you think?"

Gavin thought very definitely. "It iss a bad time we shall be having," he told us.

"A bad time? Oh, you mean the weather." The laird peered out through an arrow slot twelve inches wide and eight feet deep. "Yes. But not till evening, I'm sure." He looked thoughtful. "It may just dampen those guns a bit. What do you think, lads?"

"What about me?" Mary Hamilton asked. "I've taken two stag, and I'm not bad at birds—even Mummy says so."

Lord Inchdarroch hesitated. "I think not, Mary. This isn't a shooting expedition. It's simply a spontaneous, un-authorized, irresponsible trespass—"

"Thought up, sir," I put in, "by spontaneous, unauthor-ized, irresponsible kids."

"Yes." He looked again at Mary. "I'm afraid your mother would—er—"

"I think, Lord Inchdarroch, that you've always been afraid of my mother." With iron in her eye, Mary excused herself and left the room.

"Will it be I," Gavin asked, "to go with the young chentlemen?"

"No," said the laird. "No. Alec knows the ground perfectly. And there's really no reason why he and his friends might not call on McVittie.

"But I'm wondering a bit about the way of it. If these strangers indeed have an interest in our doings—and Major Flower thinks it possible—it will hardly do for our lads to march out in formation. Let me see. Ah—this might do. I suggest, Alec, that you take off at once for Balloch Inch—as upon errand bent. Drop in at 'The Twelve Inches.' Let yourself be seen. Then, on your way back, hide your bike in the bracken and cut across McVittie's lower ground—you should have plenty of cover—to the cove—Uig Gorm, that is. Grant and Flower here will give you half an hour's start and then go off ostensibly to fish the castle shore. They may be seen, or they may not; but they'll be quite out of sight as soon as they've rounded the point. Then it's Uig Gorm for them and a rendezvous with you.

"From which point, since you know the cover best—" he was still speaking to his son—"you must deploy troops and proceed to spy out the land. The three of you come back by water—not later than six. I fear Gavin's right about the barometer. Everything clear?"

"Excuse me, sir." For once Tommy Grant had forgotten his jive talk. "Yon's a grand scheme, but I think you should know that I'm a sair hand wi' boats. I'll not know about Posy—"

"I'm sure I can cope with the boat," I said, "but I don't have any knowledge of this water. I might not even find the cove—or whatever-you-call-it. I'm delighted to go, but I don't want to—er—goof."

"No," said his lordship. "No. We don't want—er—goofing. Tell you what: we'll send Gavin with you as far as the cove. He'll bide there with the boat till the three of you are back. Eh, Gavin? Any questions from Sir Agravaine's people—and you just stopped by to mend a thwart. Right?"

"Right, sir," said the ghillie.

An hour later I was lying in the early heather of the mountainside where Gavin Dhu had seen the strangers. "McVittie's auchter," he called the land we were on. Beside me, Alec Macnicol scanned the hills through a pair of German binoculars. Our expedition had already suffered a casualty, for poor Tommy had twisted his ankle disembarking from the boat and was in no shape for a silent crawl through hostile country. He was in considerable pain but insisted that he would stay with Gavin until our return.

"Look!" Alec breathed the word and handed me his glasses. Without disturbing the whins behind which we lay hidden, he pointed northward. On a scaur about a mile away a single figure was discernible. A gun was under his arm—I could not make out its character. He stood solidly in the rising wind and looked toward the sea.

Alec was nudging me and pointing—this time in the opposite direction. From a valley below us a stag—a fine eight-pointer—was pricking his way nervously upward, turning from time to time into the wind and breaking at last into a canter that took him out of sight.

"Somebody's down there," Alec said. "Down there and coming up, likely."

132

We crawled around our whins to another clump closer the drop-off. Far in the glen we saw him—a tall man in plus fours, moving purposefully in our direction. The vast shadow of a cloud fell over us, and from the north there was a growl of thunder.

"Aha, a third one." Alec was looking back at the first watcher. He had been joined by another. Together they began slowly to navigate the ridge that lay between them and ourselves.

"Maybe we'd better get out of here," I said. Alec's answer was lost in another thunderclap, distant but drawing nearer. He edged backward in a way that made his kilt ride up but kept him low on the horizon.

"Keep down and follow me," he whispered. I wriggled along, a little to his rear. "Any objections to a chimney?" he asked. I shook my head. The long-delayed climbing project was under way.

"Careful here." He pushed apart a clump of bristling undergrowth to disclose a fissure leading downward between screening shrubs. The extent of the crevasse was impossible to determine. The upper opening was narrow and dark, but a trickle of light showed the escarpment lower down.

"This way—in case they've spotted us—we disappear between them."

With his back against one face of rock and his feet against the other, Alec began to walk his way down the chimney. We had no rope, and I was decidedly out of practice.

"It widens here," Alec panted, "but only for a bit."

It did widen, and momentarily I doubted whether I were long enough to maintain horizontal pressure. Then the walls narrowed once more, and fifteen feet farther down we found ourselves standing on the floor of a cave. Dim light came from an opening ahead of us.

"Many's the day I've holed up here," said Alec. "You'll find chocolate and maybe biscuits in the kist yonder. Help yourself, and I'll have some too. We're bound to be late for tea."

In the gloom I saw that he was pointing to an iron coffer standing against the cave wall. Sure enough, chocolate and biscuits were in it, and regardless of their vintage we munched in satisfaction.

A crash like cannon fire slapped across the mouth of the cavern. Almost at once there was the hiss of driving rain.

"Oh, *no!*" Alec protested. "Coming from that direction, it's sure to be a big one." And indeed it was not the silent misty fall that is typical of a West Highland afternoon but a torrent—the sort of thing you would expect in the tropics.

"It's a good job we're in here—but what about the boat?" I asked. "Tommy and Gavin must be really catching it."

But the storm proved to be a front-running squall. As suddenly as it had come, the rain ceased.

"We'd best chance it," Alec advised. "Those jokers who were watching will be under any cover they can find. And there isn't much." He chuckled.

We peered from the mouth of the cave. The air was colder, and thunder continued to rumble through the mountains while great clouds blackened the tossing surface of the sea loch.

From our hiding place, a wild mass of bracken slanted downward to the water half a mile away. Everything was

soaking wet as—with a quick look around for the watchers
—we started in a crouching zigzag. We were not much worried, for by our *cheminée* we had gained quick descent and
should be many yards beyond them. Back of the shoreline
where we knew the cove to be, the sky was angry still.

Thunder stuttered and boomed again. In the moment
of silence that followed we heard the mournful whistle of
a whimbrel. Alec stood stock still. Three times the sea
bird called.

"It's Gavin," said Alec. "He's telling us where the boat
is." Used by the years to scanning miles of heather, the
ghillie's eye had picked us out against the background of
the hills.

Alec broke into a crouching lope, and I followed. Then
something whined into the earth beyond us, and from
behind there came the clang of a high-powered rifle. Another shot, and Alec threw himself into the heather.

At least I *thought* he threw himself. But when I crawled
up alongside, his voice was grimly breathless.

"I—I'm afraid I've been hit," he said.

❖ 17 ❖

I scarcely noticed the curtain of rain that swept in from the sea. I simply lay there and shook and expected the next bullet. None came.

"Is it bad?" Despite the noise of the storm, I felt compelled to whisper.

"I don't know." His voice sounded a little stronger. "It's my shoulder—the left. I'm bleeding quite a bit."

In the gloom and wet, I could see a dark stain growing across his jersey. Lightning crackled around us, and the rain was an opaque wall.

I tried to gather my stupid wits together. Ought I to leave him and go for help? In this torrent, I wasn't at all sure that I could even find the boat. As for first aid, I didn't know whether he ought to be monkeyed with— let alone moved. I listened for footsteps or action behind us: it was impossible to hear anything but the weather. By the same token, I told myself, we could not possibly be stalked.

At that precise moment, from just in front of us, a voice said, "Keep quiet."

It was a deep, soft voice, the immemorial voice of the

tracker who wishes to be heard only by those to whom he speaks.

I lay still, my hand clutching a stone.

Slowly, from a depression in the ground before us, a dark head was raised.

"Iss it that you are hurt?" It was Gavin Dhu.

I pointed to Alec's shoulder, and the ghillie crawled to where he could look closely. In the wet dark, I could barely see the rain running in channels down his face.

"He hass fainted," he said.

"Oh," I said—glumly and afraid.

"The blood"—he pronounced it "plut"—"iss not flowing fast. We shall take him to the poat. Here iss the plan." His s's were one with the rain. "See now where I am pointing. That iss your line. Stay low—ye'll know how, I think?"

"But what about Alec—what about the Master?"

"I will pring him—when you whistle that you are safe. Now go—before the rain lessens."

I realized that he had often shouldered hapless stags that weighed far more than the inert Alec. (And I was later to learn that as a sergeant with the Argyll and Sutherland, he had carried five wounded men to safety on a single night of battle.) At any rate, the sergeant's note was in his voice, and I recognized it. Taking a sight along the line he had indicated, I began to crawl—but discovered at once that because of the thickness of the weather I must revise my bearings every few yards. Since it was necessary to detour around rock clusters, I was particularly glad— after ten minutes' work—to see the gray level of the loch below me.

I had not realized how long we had been in the heather. But late as it was, there would have been in normal circumstances far more light. The Highland dusk, endless in summer, had been transformed by tempest into winter night. Greens were purple and blues were black.

But I spotted the boat, a light-colored fish on the dark belly of the shore.

"Is it you, Gavin?" Tommy Grant had spotted me in spite of my efforts at concealment.

I wormed my way through the stiff, sharp reeds. The rising hill behind me, plus the rain, perfectly screened our beachhead.

"Alec's been shot," I told him. "Gavin's bringing him down." With my mouth half full of rain, I spoke in gulps. And I was horribly embarrassed—a fat lot of good *I* had been to the expedition.

Then I remembered my instructions—and whistled, doing the whimbrel bit as best I might.

Together, Tommy and I waited, fearful lest Gavin and his burden make a target—even in the downpour.

Lightning flashed, and for an instant we saw them. I thought of posters I had looked at, especially from World War I, of heroes struggling against a shell-streaked sky.

There were no more shots, and we reached out to help Gavin with his burden.

"You young chentlemen take us out," said Gavin. "Straight so." He pointed into the rain, which for him was apparently transparent. "I shall look to this." And as the motor caught like a well-rolled "r," he took from his sporran a small hooded flashlight. He kept it off till it was close to Alec's shoulder. "The plut iss clotting," he announced after a moment. "We shall let him sleep."

But Alec was already showing signs of revival. He groaned once or twice and stirred restlessly on his improvised pallet of tarp. The rain was letting up a little.

"Keep you close to shore now, Master Tom. They can only see," said Gavin, "if we stand off."

"How's your ankle?" I whispered to Tommy.

"Like so-so. What on earth happened?"

"Tell you later, alligator"—I made so much of a concession to his idiom.

The rain stopped. But the twilight glow of a normal night was blotted out by cloud masses, still driven at a wicked pace above the chop. We crept along at half speed, unwilling to risk the sound effects of fuller power.

Alec stirred again and started to sit up. "What—where? —oh." He peered at us. "Good lads," he said, and sank back on his ruckle bed.

For a time we cruised along in comparative silence. I say "comparative" because even at half speed our bow occasionally slapped the roiling loch; but as no further action from the enemy materialized, our nerves relaxed a bit—Tommy's and mine, that is, for Gavin's, I'm sure, were iron, and Alec's, for the moment, were irrelevant.

"'Tiss ferry like the war look," said Gavin. He had shifted to the bow to give us better balance. "Inchdarroch iss dark."

Through the lifting murk, we could make out the profile of the castle, still some distance off. The bulk of the building was not wholly visible from where we looked; yet there was something strange about its appearance.

"No lights," said Tommy, and I understood what Gavin had meant by his comparison with wartime.

"The electric power," Gavin said carefully, "will have peen damaged by the storm."

Alec's voice broke in. "I say," he exclaimed in fairly normal tones, "they've blacked out home-sweet-home."

We wondered what we should find on landing and approached the water side of the castle with considerable caution.

Someone was watching, for a voice called out, "Boat there! Whose boat are you?"

"Inchdarroch's boat," said Gavin.

We made fast and climbed the high stone steps that mounted from the water. Alec insisted that he could walk and made it with some help. I gave my shoulder to Tommy Grant, and he managed to hobble the distance.

Indoors we were greeted with shock, commiseration, and first aid. Mrs. Shaw, the housekeeper, had at one time been a nurse. At her instruction, Alec was taken upstairs and put to bed, while Tommy was awarded an elastic bandage.

All this, I might add, by the light of torches, electric and otherwise. The stone-sheathed rooms were full of shadow and of the wavering light that hearth fires cast; and pine brands had been set to burn in the stairway sconces—exactly as they had burned when the castle was new.

"The storm did it," Lord Inchdarroch explained. "No power at all, and we can't even call the doctor."

We were at dinner—all of us, that is, except Alec. For him, fortunately, we had no serious concern. Mrs. Shaw—whom Gavin would not leave until he had himself checked her verdict—informed us that the bullet had furrowed Alec's shoulder, damaging flesh and muscle but not bone.

"A clean cut," she said. "He'll be no the worse in a week, though stiff maybe."

I was very glad to hear her, for a sense of despondency had come over me. The madcap capers of previous days seemed to have taken a desperate turn, and what had been almost pleasant excitement had become lost in the driving rain on the hillside above Uig Gorm. Four of us had gone out for a peep at presumable trespass, and 50 per cent of our expedition were casualties, though to be sure, Tommy's sprain might have been acquired anyhow. Furthermore, we had gained no definite impression of the marauders. It was faintly possible that they were genuine—if inept—sportsmen. On the other hand, they were unknown in the district. We were informed—*via* the backstairs—that Sir Agravaine had no visitors in residence; and his gamekeepers appeared to be curiously inactive.

"I feel very badly about this," my father said. "There's no question in my mind but that this outrage is our fault." His glance included me. "If the Flowers, *père et fils,* had not arrived at Inchdarroch, there would have been no strangers and no shooting. And I've every reason to believe that this place will have no peace while we are here." He paused. "Those shots," he said, "were undoubtedly meant for Jonathan. But the callousness with which they wounded Alec—whom they can't possibly have a grudge against—is an indication of the kind of people they are."

"We are well aware, Major," said the laird, "that you have brought us no private feud. We feel ourselves honored to serve as your billet, as it were." He laughed grimly. "It's a long time since Inchdarroch was last invested, and the walls are as strong as ever. Your glass, Major. We stick to claret in the old way. Now tell me what you conceive as the immediate prospect."

Before my father could answer, Gavin burst into the room. There were no preliminaries through the butler this time.

"It iss ringing us round they are!" He spoke with what was, for him, great excitement.

Lord Inchdarroch laid down his napkin with deliberation. "Explain yourself, man."

"Ay, I will explain. I started out to inform the pollis as you had told me to, there being no telephone this night. And I will explain that the road to Balloch Inch is blocked with two great motors back to back across the way of it. And I will explain that there iss a man in one of the motors who caught me in a light and shot at me." He drew himself up, panting. "All this I will explain."

Lord Inchdarroch showed no surprise. "A roadblock, eh? Then you never reached the police station?"

"I did not, sir."

"Where is this block, Gavin Dhu?"

"About two miles this side 'The Twelve Inches.' Moreover, I could not well make round these men through the country: there were others in the cover whose feet and breathing I could hear. There wass even a man between the road and the water."

We were all on edge now, for it seemed that the enemy was closing us in.

"They've taken advantage of the storm and know that we can't use the wires." My father spoke as if thinking aloud. "Do I understand that Gavin was to fetch the police?"

142

"Partly that. As a matter of fact, they've but two men at Balloch Inch—a sergeant and a constable. They both use bicycles, but there are several cars in the clachan. However"—his red beard wagged under a grin—"it was not the local manpower that I counted on—we're strong enough here. It was efficient action. This thing is a matter for the Chief Constable—or perhaps the Home Office, for that matter. And one thing the police station does have —power or no power—is a petrol-fired generator and a wireless."

"To send out word," said Mary Pigtail.

"Ay. To send out word—to Inverness, if need be, or to R.A.F. Kinloss. They could have a helicopter here within the hour. Or a seaplane, perhaps. These days, besides, there's been a patrol boat—out of Lochalsh, I think. She's off this land every morning about two, and we've ample anchorage."

"As things stand, how many do we number?" asked my father.

"Well asked. Let's see." The laird began to count on his fingers. "There's you and me, and the two lads here"—he indicated Tommy and me. "Alec's *hors de combat*, but of course there's Gavin and Ferguson—that's the butler. He's no hand with a gun, I'm afraid. We've twenty gamekeepers away beyond Balloch Inch, but between them and us, apparently, are these invading fellows. Our nearest recruitment would be McVittie's people. But by and large they're a sulky lot, and himself is probably snoring the snore of the just. Discounting Mary here, and Mrs. Shaw, and the maids, we've approximately six effectives—the Major, Gavin Dhu, myself—you, young Flower, Grant— and Ferguson. How's that ankle, Tommy?"

"Perfectly fit, sir," said Tom. I happened to know that it was swollen like a tire.

"I don't like being discounted," said Mary. "I've handled quite a few guns." (Yes, I thought, with silencers and bushes all about.)

The laird was most apologetic. "I didn't mean to write you off, my dear." Then he added condescendingly—and you could see the anger rise in Mary's face—"I've no doubt you can help Mrs. Shaw with Alec." He turned to the rest of us. "Always able to use a Women's Auxiliary, what?"

"But," Mary protested, "hasn't someone to get through? We can't just sit here and let them pot at us indefinitely."

"*Ex ore infantium.*" Lord Inchdarroch hitched up his chair and got down to serious briefing. "I agree," he said, "though there is some question in my mind as to timing. Did I understand you to say, Major, that a delaying action is in order—that the longer we keep these fellows busy, the surer their apprehension?"

"Something like that," said my father. "But under the circumstances, I'm not sure that they'll accept a waiting game."

"Oh—push for a showdown, eh? Well, in that case—" Lord Inchdarroch barely had the words out of his mouth when a rifle shot smashed the glass in a shoreward embrasure.

Everybody sat stock still.

"This," said Lord Inchdarroch at last, "is the absolute limit."

"Endsville," murmured Tommy Grant.

"Gavin!" The laird's voice was a roar. The ghillie stood at attention.

"Gavin Dhu, take a gun at once and cover the bridge. These men will not be swimmers, I doubt, but they might come close for some short-range nonsense. Mary, tell Mrs. Shaw to move Alec to a seaward room. There is one chance in a thousand that a shot from where they are could take accurate effect. But that's the chance we'll choose to avoid. Major, you and I will be off to the gun room. I have the key to the cases here. Arms and ammunition will be issued in five minutes." He looked concerned but eager. "If these rotten dogs keep shelling us, we'll take their pelts."

But he didn't say how. And "how" was what I had been wondering for some time, for we were quite isolated—in a situation, it was true, that was calculated for resistance but that lacked any means of communication with the rest —the decent rest—of mankind. One man with the gift of survival could defend that narrow causeway against almost any number of invaders, but no one in the castle could leave by the bridge without being instantly spotted. There was, however, enough cover on the shore side— where the road ended and we had left our car—for one or two snipers to take position and bang away at the castle in perfect safety.

It was conceivable that one of us might make a dash for it—at least as far as the Zephyr. But then I remembered Gavin's account of the roadblock, which made such a sortie useless, even if it were successful.

My brain, which is never as dependable as I could wish, was working very badly. I suppose that to some extent I was still upset by the events of the afternoon, and I know that I felt a sad responsibility for the failure of our scouting expedition. It wasn't my fault that Tommy had crocked his ankle; but I couldn't take any credit for the rescue Gavin had accomplished. It was time that the last of the Flowers made some positive contribution.

I went to the gun room. Lord Inchdarroch looked at me and handed over a fancy-looking shotgun—inlaid stock and tooled barrels.

"Know how to use this? Here's a bag of shells. Help yourself to a torch—that sealed-beam job should do. And let's see—I b'lieve we'll station you in the north tower, one flight up—my bedroom, in fact. You'll be able to watch the road. If a car comes through, don't shoot at it but fire a warning. It just might be police."

"But the police don't know. Gavin couldn't—"

"No, Gavin was a sensible chap for once. He knew his value to us here. But sooner or later someone's going to come upon that roadblock and report it"—he pulled at his beard—"unless they're shot first."

"But, sir, the road leads nowhere but here. Who would be likely—does the constable patrol this way at night?"

"Not very often, I'm afraid."

I gathered up my courage. "Then, sir, I have a request to make. May I have your permission to take the boat and run across the loch to the village—to Balloch Inch, I mean?"

He looked at me in silence.

"It's the only way to bypass them," I insisted. "With any luck at all I won't be spotted, and after I've reached the police station, the cops—the constable, that is—can bring me back."

My father coughed. "The boy's not bad with a boat, Macnicol, though maybe I'd better go with him."

"Oh no!" I said. "That would put all our eggs in one

basket. And anyway, they're after you, much more than me."

Mrs. Shaw appeared in the doorway.

"Beg pardon, m'lord. The maids is panicky. They want to go to the land, and Gavin won't let 'em. That Walker—she's the flighty one—she tried to get past him, and he's carried her back to the kitchen. I'm sure if you were to—"

"Tell them from me to go to their rooms. They're as safe as we can make them. If you think it advisable, splice the main brace."

I had forgotten that the laird had commanded H.M.S. *Tangible* in World War II.

Mrs. Shaw disappeared. Lord Inchdarroch turned back to me.

"They'll hear your engine," he said.

"It was my plan, sir, to row the first mile or so. Beyond that, they're unlikely to shoot at the sound of a motor."

The little man looked thoughtfully at my father. "It's a fair chance," he said, "and a brave offer. What do you think, Major?"

I was pretty sure what the answer would be.

"I think yes," said the Boss. "But won't he have some distance to go after he lands? As I remember, the police station is by no means on the water."

"We'll brief him fully and at once." Lord Inchdarroch took a map from one of the wall cabinets. It was easy to pick out the castle, its island base connected with the land by the slim line of causeway. Thence, to the north, the loch took shape as a sizable bay. On its farther tip stood Balloch Inch. The road moved inland to the village, and we could see by the large-scale chart that the police station was about a third of a mile from the shore.

"Here we are," said the laird. "I'll take back that gun —and give you this." He produced a small compass with phosphorescent points. "Your course from our steps will be a bit east of north. Once past the ken, you'll come to a bit *caladh*—not a real harbor but a safe enough place for beaching. There's a wide strand and then an hundred yards or so of sea grass. On you go, through the spinney to the station. They may have the electric light and they may not. In any case, their wireless will be in operation."

He told me that the sergeant, whose house was next door to the station, was himself a Macnicol—Ivor of that ilk—and that the constable's name was Ian Burden.

"Tell them you've a message from 'himself,'" he said, "and show them this."

He pulled a seal ring from the leather finger of his left-hand glove. I tried it for size, but my chunky claws were much too big for it.

"Ech now," said his lordship. "We'll put it in your sporran."

"My sporran?" I was wearing the customary flannel bags.

"Ay." He went to the door. "Mrs. Shaw," he called. "Mrs. Shaw! Come here, if you please. I want Master Alec's oldest kilt—the scout tartan will do—the Black Watch. I know it's tattered, Mrs. Shaw: the more, the better. And an old jersey, please. And the weariest sporran you can find. No, wait a minute. The lad must be a very rag bag. We'll string the ring about your neck, m'boy— along with the wee compass."

Fifteen minutes later I was the "compleat" Highland something-or-other—fisher boy, tinker—waif, at any rate. My hair, which had grown long and light during the cricket season, was thoroughly tousled, and one long lock fell over my eye. I had dirtied my face—an achievement never particularly difficult. A faded green jersey led downward to the well-worn kilt. Stockingless legs and bare feet completed the picture.

"Of course, your voice may give you away. If you have to talk before you reach the station," said the laird, "say as little as possible."

The ring and the compass felt cold against my chest. Over the loch the sky was very dark, with here and there a star shining through the cloud rack. Nowhere along the coast could I see a light: apparently the power failure was widespread. It was possible, however, to see the dim shape of the shoreline, bending to my right in an arc that ended some three miles straight ahead of me.

I have been neglectful. I ought to have described the boat in my narrative of the afternoon. She was a clinker-built dory—sixteen feet over-all, I think—of the seaworthy sort that you find on almost any British beach. Characteristically, her paint job was dark green. None of your yacht-club white for the Highlands; and I was glad of it, though the night was dark.

A small inboard engine had been installed amidships —apparently for someone who wanted to make rowing difficult, for the oarsman had perforce to sit forward or aft of the motor.

"Abaft the box, my boy!" So the laird advised, shining his torch on the dory. The castle shielded us from landward observation, and I descended the stone steps against which the loch had lapped for centuries.

"She looks heavy to row," said my father, and I thought I detected a wistful note in his usually sardonic voice.

A clutter of tarps was stowed near the engine; Alec had lain on them after the shooting. I found that the engine box made a good brace for my feet.

"Cheer-oh!" said Lord Inchdarroch.

"Luck!" said my father.

It sounded a little like a drinking bout, I thought.

The Boss threw my line into the boat, and I slipped out over the black water. The castle loomed astern like a Gothic version of Ailsa Craig. I sighted by it, and for as long as it was visible, I rowed a course due north. The loch was still choppy but less rough than in the afternoon. Except for the sound of water against the boat's bottom and, at a distance, from the landside burns in spate, there was total silence. The lack of any light along the shore added an eerie quality to the intermittent starshine.

Ordinarily, in my opinion, physical exercise dulls the imagination. When I run the mile, I am usually aware of nothing more than rhythm, kick, and wind. I know golfers, too, who can shut out everything but the game in hand. One of my Argentinian friends boasts that when he is putting, he would probably not notice cannon fire. (My father has described to me golf at Fort Benning during World War II when the pattern of the course was used as a mock target for low-flying bombers.)

Perhaps rowing requires less concentration. Whatever the reason, I had rowed somewhat less than a mile when a strange sense of apprehension overtook me. I wasn't afraid of the water; I wasn't afraid of the dark; I wasn't afraid of being alone. But somehow the combination of circumstances made me feel what the British—with a meaning quite different from our own—call "nervy."

I thought I saw fish in the whitecaps. I remembered the

"dark riders" that haunted Stephen Crane. The cloud mass personified itself as Dr. Fisher-Finch, bowler-hatted and bulky of shoulder. . . . And then the crumpled tarp pile, astern of the motor, moved.

I broke stroke for the moment, then told myself it was the wind.

But it wasn't.

While I watched in fascinated horror, the folds of rubber cloth and dark green canvas took on bulk and body. Something was moving under the ruck of waterproof. The stuff bulged upward—dim starshine gave the canvas life and an emerging shape. A dark head appeared.

❖ 18 ❖

"Hello, Posy," said a friendly voice.

It was, of course, Mary Pigtail.

"I'm sorry, Posy, but I simply refuse to be confined to nursing. Tops for Miss Nightingale—but not for me. So, here I am."

"You scared the pants off me," I said.

"How indelicate!" There was a shiver in her voice.

"I fear, Miss Hamilton," I told her, "that I am lost to considerations of delicacy." I meant it. "This is a rough expedition, and what earthly good your presence will contribute—" I realized that I was being less than cordial. "May I ask what gives?"

"You sound like Tommy Grant," said Mary. "If nothing else gives, at least you have company."

That much I could admit.

"Aren't you going to use the motor?" she asked. "We must be out of earshot now."

"My dear girl," I told her, "I have a picture of the whole shore picketed by villains. And deary me, I've lost my sights."

Indeed, from the moment of Mary's apparition, I had

lost track of any and all bearings. I reached inside my jersey and fished for the compass.

"That," said Mary, gazing skyward, "is the North Star. I saw the front end of the Dipper a minute ago. Stick with it, Posy."

"To tell the truth," I admitted, "I'm not at all sure how you start this infernal machine. I'm all right with outboards, but has this thing got a starter? I seem to recall that Gavin used a crank."

"Imbecile!" She gave the word a French pronunciation. "Here. Let me."

A moment later—and without much snort—we were churning along at a good four knots.

"*Rami super mare quiescunt*"—Mary's scansion was better than mine. We peered at the shore, but there was no reaction to our motor music.

"Permission to speak, Captain Hornblower?" She was scarcely apologetic for the fright she had given me.

"Permission granted, Mr.— What was that lieutenant's name? Briggs, wasn't it?"

"No, not Briggs. It was Christian."

"You're nuts," I said. "Christian was on the *Bounty*. You know—'Mr. Christian! Mr. Christian!'" I gave my almost perfect rendering of Charles Laughton's voice.

"You've no need to shout, Captain Bligh. Israel Hands is in the mizzentop with a marline spike in his fist—or I'm much mistaken." She emitted what, in a lesser girl, would have been called a giggle. "I admire your get-up, Posy. You look like the female lead in 'The Little Minister'."

"Stop being so literary," I said. "Have you any idea

where we are?" The motor burbled quietly onward, and an occasional swell hit our bow with a slap.

"You've failed a bit in your dead reckoning, Captain H. Yes, I know exactly where we are. I'm up here every summer, more or less. I suggest that we cut the engine and resort once more to the sweeps. Good heavens! You *do* look like the Idiot Boy!"

A slice of moonlight had shot for an instant through the cloud bank. Mary, I surmised, had stowed away before my costuming had been completed.

She cut the motor, and we dawdled briefly on the impetus of former power.

"We're about two hundred yards off the *caladh*," she said, "harbor, to you. There's pretty decent sand all about here, and no surf to speak of."

I couldn't help it. I said:

"But now I only hear
Its melancholy, long, withdrawing roar."

She was with it (as Grant would say): "'Dover Beach,' my eyeballs!" Then, in a Mammy Yocum voice, "Whar'd you get sich larnin', son?" Her good-school accent came back in a flash. "Easy on the oars, Captain. *Nous y sommes.*"

I had really had enough of this bookish bravado—or so I took it to be—and I was glad to hear the gentle grating of our boat on the beach. I hopped out into two or three inches of very cold water, and we pulled up on the shingle.

Everything around us was quiet and dark.

"The laird said that the police station was about a third of a mile."

' Yes,' she said.

I decided to ground her.

"You stay here," I said.

"I will not." Her tone was metallic. "We're leaving the boat behind, aren't we? You said the P.C. would drive you back—"

I'd forgotten that. My orders were to return with the cops. But to tell the truth, I wasn't particularly happy about claiming an SOS credit. "Sparks, the fearless boy-officer"—that sort of thing. On the other hand, obviously I couldn't let her go back alone, and she was determined, it appeared, not to stay with the boat.

"We may get spotted," I said (though at the time, I didn't think so). "Give me a thirty second start to reconnoiter. If I run into trouble, I'll yell—in which case don't try to find *me*. Find the police station."

It wasn't very gallant, I admit. Nor was the reasoning by which I hoped to make it through the spinney well ahead of any pigtails. But she acquiesced.

The beach was broad and the sand firm. I wiggled my toes and hoped there weren't many thistles up ahead. The sea grass cut me once or twice, but inside of a minute I had reached the grove of trees and was groping my way through a darkness more intense than any I had met before. There was no point in looking back for Mary, and quite literally, I had to feel my way.

About fifty yards in, I brought up against a tree with a wind-jarring smack. Whether it was the sound of collision or the grunt that came out of me, I don't know. But off to my right, a torch sprang into business, swept past me with its white beam, hesitated, and came back to rest on my tattered kilt. The torch's owner was very nearby.

"You boy, there—who are you?" The accent was anything but Scottish.

There was no point in my running. I could hardly avoid the light, and in the alternative dark I was sure to knock myself out against a tree. The light drew nearer. Desperately, I tried to hit on a suitable stratagem: the torchbearer might be an enemy—probably was—or he might be a policeman. It was hardly likely that anyone else would be wandering about in the remnants of the storm. I resolved on the boldest ploy I could think of.

"Lord, ha' mercy!" I shrieked it in my highest tones and broadest brogue. (The shout, I hoped, would take care of Mary.) "Kelpies winna' hurt puir Tam," said I, crossing myself in what I hoped was a picture of peasant panic. And having gone so far, I immersed myself further, by gesture and speech, in the role of the Idiot Boy—as kindly suggested by Miss Hamilton.

I pulled at my forelock, and with vague recollections of *Lear*, I heard myself quoting:

"Tam will throw his head at them. Avaunt, you curs!"

This announcement left the light bearer unmoved. From what I could see of him behind his torch, he was heavy of figure and topped by a cap.

"Who are you, kid? Where'd you come from?"

I peeped at him shyly between fingers held over my eyes.

"Puir Tam," I said. "None hurts puir Tam." Then, waxing bolder in view of his Sassenach speech, I let him have what is just about my total Gaelic: *"Srioghal mo dhream,"* I said. "Puir Tam. *An cirean Ceann Cinnidh!* Puir Tam." Then I burst out laughing in an attempt at eldritch lunacy.

"Cor!" exclaimed my interlocutor. "Over here, Loogan." He was summoning a colleague and called in a voice that was just short of shouting. "I've caught a weirdie, I have."

There was a sound of snapping branches and a heavy tread in our direction. I kept on peering through my parted fingers and muttering little gems about "puir Tam."

The newcomer entered the circle of light. "Where'd *he* come from?" he asked. The conversation of these two was somewhat limited.

"From the water, looks like. Where'd you come from, kid?"

"Puir Tam," I said. "Achnashellach. Drumnadrochit." (Unless they were a lot more familiar with Scotland than I thought, place names would do as well as anything else.)

"Don't he speak no English?" Number Two sounded irritated. "Speak English, kid. What's your name? Where you from?"

I decided to conciliate them. "Puir Tam's a fisher lad." I giggled at this revelation and added, "Ardnamurchan."

They looked at each other.

"Puir Tam's daft," I said. "None hurts puir Tam."

"Nuts. He's nuts." Number Two was observant. "That's what he is—nuts."

I bowed and kissed my hand.

"Where are you going, kid?" It was obvious that these were pickets, guarding the right wing of the encirclement.

I began to whistle—"The Flowers of the Forest," I think it was.

"Shut up," said Number One. "Maybe we better show him to the Dutchman."

I didn't like the sound of that, but Number Two promptly took a load off my mind.

"The Dutchman has enough to think about. They're moving in tonight. I been waiting for word right along." He tried once more. "Where you going, kid?"

"Puir Tam," I said, and—reverting to Shakespeare— " 'Come o'er the bourn, Bessy, to me.' "

For some reason, it made me think of Mary, and I wondered how much of this flash-lit chat she was taking in. Number Two ended my meditation with a kick at the rear of my kilt.

"Get along, kid. And bear in mind—if you've got one —you ain't seen a soul—get it?"

I got it.

And—as we used to say at Lower Merion—I *got*.

The torch went black behind me as I whiffled through the spinney. Where Mary was I could not know. A whistle shrilled, and I suspected that One and Two were being hailed to active duty. Mary—what would she do? Ought I to cut back through the wood to find her? With characteristic lack of gallantry, I thought not. If she had any sense, she'd go back with the boat. There was, I told myself, very little likelihood that One and Two would resume their off-beat patrol.

As for my own errand, the sooner I got out of those woods, the better.

The sky continued to abstain from real moonlight. There was, however, enough of starshine here and there —or my eyes had grown sufficiently used to the darkness —for me to sense an eastward course and take off through the trees. There was no light that I could see in the direction of the village, but as I neared the road, a faint gleam or two denoted lamps or glowing hearths.

After about ten minutes stumbling, I broke from cover and found myself on the loch side of a line of cottages. As for the police station, I'm not sure what I expected in the way of identification. There certainly were no neon signs or double lampposts. I stood outside a dark but not dingy-looking cottage—then ducked back around the angle of the house as a thin beam of light came tumbling down the street.

That's the only way I can describe it, though I recognized it quickly as the headlamp of a bike. Uncertain whether or not this was another marauder, I kept to the inky shadow. But the reflection of his light from the white walls of the cottage showed up a man in dark-blue uniform.

I sprinted after him, cobbles and pebbles whacking at my toes.

"Constable!" I puffed—I dared not shout. "Officer! Policeman!"

He skidded to a stop.

"What's this?" The beam from his torch haloed me around. "Who may you be?" (It was getting a bit monotonous.)

His voice was worried and annoyed.

I decided it was time to forget about daft Tammie. "Are you Sergeant Macnicol?" I asked. "I've a most important message." A mild amount of Scots stuck to my tongue.

He had dismounted. "Constable Burden here." He was not, apparently, resolved to produce handcuffs. "Who are you, lad?"

"I'm from the laird, Constable—from himself." I was far from sure how to describe my authorization. "I've a message for the sergeant—or for you." I lowered my voice. "Inchdarroch's in trouble."

He gave me a long look. "Ay, I know thiss. The power's awa'. The storm did it. 'Tis the fate of such as depend on the electricity." He gave a hitch to his tunic. "Aweel, if you've a word for the sergeant, we'll gae together. This way, laddie. It's been a curious night, this night. I doubt the sergeant's at the station. Come away, however—we'll knock him up somewhere about."

So we did.

The sergeant was at his own house but not yet asleep —although it was well past midnight. I can't say he was very glad to see us—he huffed and puffed on a nightcap pipe and expressed amazement at what I had to tell. To begin with, I think, he suspected me of being an American prankster; but my presentation of Inchdarroch's ring changed him from a skeptic to a strong support.

"I can hardly believe it," he said. "Yet I know there's been strangers on McVittie's land these few days." He shrugged a shade apologetically. "McVittie's at home, ye'll mind. And he's no love for the pollis. We'd scarce intrude—"

"I know what you mean," I told him, "and so does Lord Inchdarroch. But the fact is, these strangers have us cut off. They're between you here and the castle. And they've blocked the road with a couple of cars."

He looked—if possible—embarrassed. "Ian," he said, "have ye been down that way the night?"

"I've not," said the constable. "I was right on my way when—"

"When I stopped him," I put in, and—under the impression that we had spent enough time in explanations and apologies—"I understand, sergeant, that you've no regular electricity. But the laird—Lord Inchdarroch, I mean—said that your radio worked off a generator, with independent power."

"Ay," said the sergeant. "It does so."

"What I mean to say is—he expects you to send for—er—assistance—to Inverness or whatever's the nearest spot where there'd be manpower to move in against these mobsters. By air—or possibly the patrol boat—"

I broke off: the sergeant was looking at me so fiercely. (I have neglected to say that he was a rather small person, with an air of eager pugnacity.)

"Assistance?" He barked the word at me. "Assistance? I scarcely think it's come to that, my lad. The present force"—he embraced Constable Burden in his glance—"the present force has coped with a number of situations, during the war and since. Syne there was but one here—"

He hesitated, looked sidewise at the constable, and went on—a little less rapidly. "To be sure, times change, and we now have what is called centralization." I expected a political harangue, but he went on, his mind apparently made up. "We'll just let them know, away there—" He was taking some wooden tees from his pocket and stopped short in the act. Then he waved one in what might have been the direction of Inverness.

"How many of these incomers did ye say there were?"

"At least eight," I ventured. "There were two or three on the hillside—and that pair I met tonight. And I know of others who haven't actually appeared—"

"Aweel," he said. "We'll send in a report and then

make for Inchdarroch." He looked me up and down. "Ye'll be cold, laddie," he said. "Here, missus, a cuppa for this lad. No?" (I said, "Yes, thank you.") "Meanwhile, I'm for the station."

I told him I'd like to see his wireless set-up, and he said that I might come along. Tea could wait.

The radio was a self-sustaining operation, working on batteries that were supplied by a gasoline generator. What with signals squawking of bad weather and low ceilings, it took the sergeant a good half hour to reach his headquarters. I expected him at least to ask for reinforcements—but not Sergeant Macnicol.

"Spot of trouble here," he said—after a mysterious exchange of code letters and acknowledgments. "Team o' roughs about Inchdarroch, so it seems. Reported armed. Poachers, probably. Taking Constable Burden with me. What? Ay, my responsibility. Source of information?" He looked at me with what I am sure he would have described as dubiety. "Source apparently reliable. I'll pick you up later, right?"

"But, Sergeant," I said, "the whole point of my coming over here was to get reinforcements. Lord Inchdarroch realizes—I'm sure he has every confidence in your ability —but Lord Inchdarroch realizes, just as I do, that even you and the constable can't take on this gang. They're all armed—with rifles, we think, and—"

The little sergeant bristled. "Correction," he said, speaking into the microphone. "Constable Burden will remain on duty here. I have instructed him"—he looked across at my friend of the bicycle—"I have instructed him to remain on local duty. Ay, sir. Ay, sir. We'll be sure to let you know." There was a pause. "No. They've no phone the night."

He plunked the microphone back in its bracket. "All right, young man, we'll see about these fancy lads."

I was appalled. Whatever criminal conditions there might usually be in Balloch Inch, I was certain that the sergeant had no notion of the situation now existing at Inchdarroch. I could not see him—even with *my* modest help—handling the troop of international hoods I pictured at the castle.

And back of these misgivings, I began to wonder—belatedly, I admit—about Mary Pigtail and the strangers in the spinney. Surely she would have had sense enough, after my yell, to go back to the boat.

"Really, Sergeant," I began.

But he cut me off. "There's a wee line in your telly shows—American, I mean—that I've liked fine. 'Time's a-wastin'.'" With great determination he thrust his pipe into his pocket. "We'll be away now. Fetch the car, Ian. And once it's brought, bide you here."

We climbed into a rather ancient Humber.

"Sergeant," I said. "There's a girl—down on the beach, I think. She came along with me. I didn't ask her: she just stowed away on the boat. I don't want to leave you, but I'm afraid I'll have to go back and make sure she's all right."

I could hear his puff of impatience. "A girl, is it?" he snorted. "Pray how does a girl stow away in a boat you've described as sixteen-foot?" I made no answer. "And *which* is more important, Master Messenger—that the rogues be nabbed at Inchdarroch or that we rescue your sweetie who's stravagin' through yon spinney?"

163

I didn't care much for this line of talk. "She's not my sweetie," I told him. And then—really, I think, because I had a lot of confidence in Mary Pigtail's ability and considerably less in the sergeant's—"All right," I said. "We'll forget about her for the moment, though I can't say I like it."

You will observe that this is no tale of chivalry. While there was time, I ought probably to have jumped from the moving car and plunged into the thicket. To tell the truth, once we left the station, I was none too sure of my whereabouts, and there was every likelihood that searching for Mary would mean getting lost myself. I have wondered often since that night how things might have turned out if I had insisted on leaving the sergeant or persuaded him to join me in a girl hunt. Ah well—as the Boss says, "You never know at the time."

✤ 19 ✤

There are two hills on the shore road from Balloch Inch, one about half a mile from the village and the other some-what closer to the castle. The sergeant shifted down to top the first, and beyond the fan of the headlights I saw a curi-ous red glow in the sky.

"What's that?" I asked. "Northern lights?"

The sergeant jammed his foot on the brake pedal. "Northern lights? It iss not." He flicked the switch on the dashboard for a better look, and we eased along the hill-crest through a darkness that blushed uneasily ahead of us.

"That's fire, m'lad. Fire's what that is." He switched our car lights on again, and we began to move at rather more speed—so I thought—than the bumpy Highland track would allow.

Suddenly I remembered the roadblock. Two miles to-ward the castle from "The Twelve Inches," Gavin had said.

"What about the barrier, Sergeant—the cars across the road?" We were swooping down now into a valley between the hills. The fire glow seemed to be brightening on the horizon.

The sergeant chuckled. "Illegal barricade of traffic is chargeable," he said.

Then we saw them—two big black closed cars, like hearses, back to back across the road.

"Careful," I said. "They shot at Gavin."

"Ay."

But he did not turn our lights off. On the contrary, as he slowed the Humber, he fixed the blockade in a spotlight that jutted from beside our windshield. I must confess that I took one look and ducked, expecting a barrage at any second.

Nothing happened.

"Either they've skipped, or they're down below the windows." The sergeant's voice was grim. "There's nae bloody sign of them."

We stopped.

"You stay here." He was pulling his rank now.

The door of the Humber snicked open, and Sergeant Macnicol was on the ground, monkeying with the spot.

He played it to-and-fro, the length of the two big cars. His challenge was one for the books: "Ye'll come out now, please—if ye're in there!"

No answer.

"Ye'll come out—noo!" Again there was no answer, and with—what was it? stupidity or heroism?—he advanced on the blockade.

I held my breath as he calmly took a torch from his pocket and shined it onto the driver's seat of the left-hand limousine. (Both cars were all of that, with glass windows between the chauffeur and his passengers.)

He moved over to the other Daimler.

Without turning to me, he barked out, "Skipped! And

just for our convenience, left the keys. Come over here, young Lochinvar. Can you manage a motor?"

I told him I could and edged rather gingerly out of the Humber. It seemed to me that his examination of the scene had been what the books call "cursory."

"Back this one up yon bank. We'll proceed between them."

I did as I was told, wishing that I might have more time with those super-smooth controls.

"Tell you what," said the sergeant. "Wait till I'm through. Then put her back. Might as well make them think everything's as they left it."

I couldn't follow his reasoning. If anything, we should be blocking reinforcements. But I didn't argue. The Humber rolled through the opening. I put my super wagon back in its blockading spot, and we continued down the valley.

"As I see it," I said—for I felt that this lionheart beside me needed some advice—"they've advanced on the castle. One of those men in the spinney said something about 'moving in'." I looked ahead. "Good gravy!" I said. "Do you think they've set fire to the causeway?"

"It wudna burn."

But we both stared with apprehension at the orange-red that flowered in the sky's end.

We ran through the dip and began to climb the second hill. Up and up on the narrow track with that false dawn growing brighter beyond us.

We reached the top.

"I'll not believe it," said Sergeant Macnicol. "I'll not believe it. Never I will!"

The stretch of the loch that lies right before Inchdarroch was in sight; the low shore acres were colored an intermittent pink and black. The castle itself rose, grimly visible; and in the crisscross cauldron of the beacon basket, high on the outer tower, a great blaze burned—six or eight feet of fire, I made it—with reflections that were bloody ribbons flowing out to sea.

"He's done it!" The sergeant's foot was firm on the brake. "Macnicol has done it—he's called the people!"

"The signal to the clansmen?"

"Ay. Ay, laddie. That flame last was up for Queen Victoria's Golden Jubilee. And before that—for the 'Forty-five, I'll warrant. He's mad, that man. But he must be fair desperate—"

"What'll happen?"

"Less than he hopes, I'm sure."

We were rolling down the hill now, our headlights adding to the offbeat spectrum of colors. A pinch of dawn lay in the east; for the rest it was the final scene in *Die Walküre.*

I knew that we must be nearing the forces of encirclement. Indeed, we were now within five hundred yards of the causeway.

Then—I swear it—the sergeant let go the wheel, stood up in his place, and emitted a yell that would have frightened an Iroquois.

The car lurched off line, and I caught the wheel trying to reach the brake with my foot. The maniac policeman kept screaming at the top of his lungs.

"Look!" he shrieked. "Look there! McVittie's out! They've caught them in the midst! They've caught them fair! Look—man and man!"

In the whins to our right, I heard the thrashing sound

of struggle. Ahead of us a tumbling, wrestling pair came reeling onto the road, one in a kilt, the other—making heavy work—enveloped in a raincoat.

The sergeant stopped screaming and halted the car. His spotlight swept the ground before the causeway. A shot rang out from the castle gate—Gavin on guard, I thought. Opposite him on the mainland, two more contestants were exchanging haymakers. A pistol cracked, and there was yelling of two sorts: the terror-stricken yowl of city hoodlums and the war cry—it could be nothing else—the war cry of embattled Highlanders. All over the castle foreland, free-for-all bouts were splashed with firelight and shadow.

From the slope at our left a pipe began to play—and another. It was a mighty pibroch—"The Highland Brigade at Mons," I think. I verily felt that my hair was rising on my scalp.

The spotlight swung to a knoll above the land end of the bridge, and we saw the principal person of this foray. A great fat Scot, red of face save for white cat-mustaches, stood, legs braced wide apart, kilt flying in the early morning wind. He was in full Highland dress, including a spectacular white sporran. Over his mighty shoulder hung a targe, the like of which you only see on walls. In his right hand was an enormous basket-hilted broadsword, and with his left he raised a great stone bottle to his lips.

Between shouts, that is, for over the tumult, his voice, like a rolling Russian bass, trumpeted out in motley exhortation.

"Oh, Stanley, on! Strike at him, Colin! Strangle the base baboon! Kick him in the teeth, man!" At about this point in the sequence, he would pause for a draught from the bottle—only to resume at once, waving the broadsword in ferocious, glittering circles around his head. "Prize it, McVittie!"—it was, I gathered, a family slogan. "Forward, ye kerns and gallowglasses!"—he was the classic stentor.

> "Come one, come all—this rock shall fly
> From its firm base as soon as I!"

And having treated us to these souvenirs of the schoolroom, he broke into "Glory, glory, hallelujah!"

As a matter of fact, nobody in his right mind would have risked the wild sweep of that broadsword, for the wrath of Sir Agravaine McVittie was terrible to see—as well as hear.

"Prize it, McVittie!" Though the cry reminded me regrettably of biscuits, I could only admire the old man's energy—"Bash them, boys, bash them!"

The sergeant and I made our way toward the chieftain. At the same time a bare-chested ghillie, blood on his face from an ugly cut, came half dragging, half dangling a badly damaged victim—presenting his prey, as it were, to his master. Sir Agravaine dropped his sword and grasped the reeling prisoner by the collar of his raincoat. Turning to my friend in blue, the old laird spoke in the most casual of voices.

"Morning, Sergeant. Delightful day. Here's one for you." Sir Agravaine raised his bottle and applied it in a swinging arc to his captive's head. He then let go the inert human bundle and returned to conversation.

"Only one or two succeeded in using their guns. I told the laddies to take their weapons first. Then them." Another victim was brought to his attention. Scarcely interrupting his remarks, he administered another *coup de*

grâce and went on. "Jolly good of Macnicol to fire the beacon. Didn't know old stiff-lips had the guts—I beg your
pardon, Sergeant; of course you're one of his. Pity you
people live so far away. Don't know when I've had as
pleasant a morning." He raised the bottle and took a considerable pull.

One by one, additional victims were brought to Sir
Agravaine's notice. In each case the sergeant, from an
apparently inexhaustible store, produced handcuffs and
applied them. One ghillie reported with a sprained
shoulder, and the chieftain cheered him with a jolt of
uisge beatha. "Well done, Ruadh," said Sir Agravaine.

The sky was brightening in the east and the beacon fire
dropping into paler color. Over the causeway crept a new
variety of tints, and back of McVittie's hills there was a
patch of blue in the morning sky.

"Five, six, seven, eight," said the sergeant. "That'll be
the lot, yess?" He seemed to be asking me.

"I don't know, Sergeant," I said. "There was the man
who was at 'The Twelve Inches.' I'd know him, I'm sure.
And he's not in this bunch." I waved a bare and dirty foot
at the heap of prisoners. All of them were more or less
affected by the impact of Sir Agravaine's bottle. "He's the
top man, actually—at least, I think so."

I was pleased that Sir Agravaine didn't ask who I was
but seemed to take me for granted as the sergeant's asso-
ciate.

A gruff voice broke in on our conference.

"Pegging your pardon, chentlemen: the laird's compli-
ments, and breakfast is served."

Sir Agravaine clapped me across the shoulders, and the
bottle in his hand nearly cracked my ribs.

"I call that handsome," he said. "First he gives us sport, and then he entertains us. Tell him, my man, that we'll be right along—as soon as we've disposed of these blasted pacifists. Colin, do you fetch the pick-up lorry and help the sergeant load his prisoners—no, I've a better idea. Carry 'em over the bridge and we'll pop 'em into Inchdarroch's dungeon. Gad now, what's a dungeon for? After all, there are several sorts of hospitality. All right with you, Sergeant?"

"Quite right, Sir Agravaine. We've but the one cell at the station."

I doubt if I'll ever forget the strange parade that followed. Eight stout McVittie ghillies had each his man, slung sackwise like dead deer across his shoulders, and in single file we made our way over the bridge to the castle gate.

Standing in the doorway was Miss Mary Hamilton.

Mary's part in the night's adventure was the chief topic at the breakfast table. Everybody thought I was a good lad, et cetera, to have got through the lines, and Sir Agravaine laughed long and loud over my imitation of the village idiot. But it was Mary's enterprise that won the major plaudits.

"There's been wood stacked under the battlements for years," said Mary. "I've noticed it often; and while it's not terribly dry, it got right along when I'd added the petrol."

Lord Inchdarroch interrupted. "You knew about the gate, then?"

"In the side of the beacon? Oh yes. As a matter of fact, sir, I've thought about calling the clans from that tower ever since—ever since my first visit when I was ten."

Our host made a sound of dubious approval.

"You see," Mary went on, "when I heard Posy screech after we'd landed, I'd a pretty good idea he'd been taken. So I said to myself"—she paused to insert a slice of toast and marmalade—"I said to myself: 'The snatch is on'— wouldn't that be right, Posy?—and I decided I'd be more useful here."

She might have hung around a bit, I thought; but remembering that when the chance came I had not gone to look for her, I made no comment.

"It was a bit of a push getting the boat back in the water," Mary said, "but once aboard the lugger—"

"You had no trouble with the engine?" my father asked. "I've found that when Posy's had his mitts on a motor—excuse me, son—"

"Oh, none at all, Major Flower." Mary smiled sweetly at the Boss. "I rather think our outbound voyage had tuned things up. Of course I *did* miss masculine assistance." The smile, this time acidulous, was beamed at me. Altogether, I wasn't coming off very well.

"Anyway," said Mary, helping herself to another sausage, "before I was halfway back, I thought of the beacon. And by the way, gentlemen, d'you realize that the castle was completely undefended from the loch side? Anyone could have landed there."

"Oh groovy," said Tommy Grant, who was sitting with his swollen ankle propped up on a chair, and who, having but lately risen, was cross about his short share in the night's adventure.

"Confident, were you, Inchdarroch?" Sir Agravaine poured the last of his bottle into a cup of tea. "Ah well, as long as *I* was in residence—ah yes, I understand. I will say, though, that I scarcely believed young Rennie when he woke me with word of the fire." He looked around the table and drew a deep and aromatic breath. "Must admit I've seldom had a more enjoyable morning."

"Anyone could have landed there," Mary repeated. "And your interior guard wasn't very much. I suppose everyone was at the windows. At any rate I wasn't stopped all the way up the battlements. And then—"

"And then—?" Lord Inchdarroch's question was kindly.

"And then I simply lit the fire—and waited."

"Jolly good show," said Sir Agravaine. "Where's that man of yours, Macnicol? I want—"

"Ferguson," said his lordship, "bring Sir Agravaine a bottle of Laphroaig, or should you rather have Talisker, McVittie?"

"Anything to swim the kippers, Inchdarroch."

"And one of your men, Sir Agravaine, decided that intervention was appropriate?" It was the sergeant speaking. Since depositing his prisoners in the dungeon, he had no doubt busied himself with porridge and black pudding.

"Quite right, too." Sir Agravaine had the new bottle before him. "Neighbors for centuries. Foes for years. Friends overnight. How's that, m'lord?" Ceremoniously, if a shade out of balance, our rescuer rose to his feet. "Give him an Inch," he said.

The laird rose opposite. Like magic, Ferguson was at his elbow with a cow's-horn quaich, silver trimmed. Disregarding his teacup, Lord Inchdarroch reached for the bottle and toasted his guest. "Prize it, McVittie," he said.

Lest you should think, however, that breakfast degenerated into a drinking bout, I must report that Sir Agravaine was shortly upon his rotund way, lustily singing "Hey, Johnnie Cope" as he crossed the causeway, whirling his broadsword about his head. He was cheerily surrounded by his faithful followers.

Without anybody's urging I went to bed—to be wakened some hours later by an unexpected sound, the ringing of the telephone. At the same time, through my open window, I heard the unmistakable moan of a steam whistle.

By the time I had gotten myself downstairs, the castle was full of news. The power lines had been repaired; the telephone was working; Balloch Inch had called the sergeant to say that Inverness was flying over an inspector; the patrol boat had cast anchor in Padraich's Harbor; and a number of Inchdarroch tenants had come in from their crofts reporting the shore road free of obstacles—and lamenting their absence from the morning's battle. Our prisoners, I learned, had been trucked away under charges of trespass, illegal possession and use of arms, and a profusion of offenses under Scottish law. Among the accused, my father said, were a number of known agents. To our annoyance, there was no word of the doctor.

Almost as soon as I had absorbed the tidings, a seaplane landed on the loch, and a boat came ashore from H.M. Corvette *Symington*. The rest of the day was a festival of statements, inquiry, reassurance, and congratulations.

To our usual company at dinner, there were added the inspector and his pilot—plus Lieutenant MacCargo (commanding *Symington*). Sir Agravaine McVittie had been asked by messenger, but word was returned that the chieftain, slightly indisposed, had taken to his bed.

The meal was magic and the menu one of those marvels that you tell yourself could not possibly be produced in the wilds of the West Highlands. The epic revelry of breakfast was beyond recapture; the tension of the night before was gone; but restored electricity gave us a sense of security and appetite. The Boss tells me that I am over-addicted to eating, so I shan't belabor the details. Suffice it to say that nearing the close of the orgy, I drew a long sigh, and Mary, who was seated on my right, remarked in her bonniest Mayfair, "I say, I'd no idea you were so revoltingly gutsy!"

We were all tired and we all went early to our beds—without a care in the world.

A little after midnight, a grenade smashed three low windows in the western approach.

My father beckoned me to his room an hour or so later. There had been no one hurt, but alarums and excursions had involved us all. The laird was furious; the lieutenant had offered a bevy of men and machine-guns; the inspector had fumed into the telephone with orders for Balloch Inch and reports to Inverness. Mary had appeared, looking very pigtailish indeed in a long white wrapper.

"Shall we fire the beacon again?" she asked.

"We'll no such thing." Lord Inchdarroch was emphatic. "This is the doing of a maniac. There's nothing in it for us until morning."

And it was after that that everyone decided to go back to bed. The enemy had apparently tossed his contraption from the causeway. Poor, patient Gavin was posted in the arrow slot—once more—above the bridge. Lord Inchdarroch gave him the largest torch we had—a spotlight, really. But it was in a mood rather different that we made for bed this second time.

And then, as I say, my father beckoned me to his room. "Tomorrow we'll be off," he said.

I didn't know what he meant. "Off? You mean we're leaving?"

"Not exactly," he answered. "I mean that we came up

here to do some climbing, and some climbing we shall do."

"But considering the bomb business—"

He cut me off. "It's the bomb business that makes our jaunt imperative. Don't you see? You and I are the magnets, the drawing cards, the targets of these attacks. We can't let Inchdarroch take all this on our account. His other guests are endangered; he himself is put to no end of inconvenience; the whole neighborhood's in an uproar —on account of you and me."

"Is it your idea that the wicked are still out there in force?" If they were, I thought to myself, the Boss and I would be walking right into their clutches.

"Not in force," he said. "Most of them went off this morning in the truck. But your friend the doctor— van Hoost or whatever we choose to call him—he's still at large. And still vindictive. Witness tonight."

"You think he planted the grenade?"

"I think he threw it. The man's incredible. I think he threw it from the causeway and that he's probably listening outside our window now—riding a broomstick, if necessary. I think he'll keep on making a menace of himself until he gets his way with us—or, more reasonably, until he forces information out of me with which he can bargain for his freedom." The Boss drew a lengthy sigh. "The thing has boiled itself down to a man-to-man issue. But first I must draw him away from Inchdarroch. And I'd leave you here—if I might—but I honestly believe that they'll be safer without either of us—and you'll be safer with me; and"—he gave me a long, odd look—"and I'll be safer with you."

There wasn't very much that I could say about this solemn declaration. "Where'll we go?" I asked.

"Time enough tomorrow for that." (I detest these wavings-off by superior adults—even when they're as superior as the Boss. However, he mitigated the offense.) "Tomorrow nothing." He was looking at his watch. "In four or five hours. To bed now. I'll call you."

I don't know whether anybody has been interested enough to count up the hours of sleep I had aggregated in the few days past, but for some strange reason I felt fresh as a daisy—or should I say Posy?—when his fist beat on the door.

It was a glorious morning. The bright, clean air was made up of salt from the sea and perfume from the bracken and the budding heather. A cool breeze blew from the north, and we set our faces to it as the sun lingered low behind the mountains and gulls flew white over our heads.

✤ 21 ✤

We took the shore road first, seeing no one about; but before we reached the clachan, the Boss swung us to the right, pursuing the banks of a very busy burn.

"This," my father explained, "is the end of McVittie's holding. We'll cross in a mile or so to where Macnicol holds a finger in the hills. Then we'll be on crown land as far as Glenwhistle. It occurred to me that you might like to see Loch Auber—the original 'dank tarn' you know—"

I knew about "Ulalume" all right—but something else was principally on my mind.

"How on earth can we draw him off if he didn't even see us leave?"

My father laughed. "He saw us all right. If I'm not mistaken, he's less than half a mile behind. He'd have no difficulty tracking us this far—he's no Deerslayer, but he was brought up on the veld. In any case, let's give him a run for his money. It's here we start climbing—and I daresay our wind's a bit better than his."

We began to slant up the vacant treeless face of a sizable mountain.

"Ben Cockie," he explained. "He'll see us now, but he won't when we've rounded the scaur."

The footing, initially soft at the burn side and springy thereafter, and the green slope of the mountain gave way, bit by bit, to rock and rubble.

We were well up now, having covered, by my estimate, six or seven miles from Inchdarroch. The bright morning stayed with us—flat white clouds across the northern blue, into which, like a clipper prow, Ben Cockie knifed its scaur. Far below, the sea ran off to the west, and in misty shapes on the horizon I fancied that I saw the Outer Hebrides.

But down the sweep of the mountainside no moving thing was visible. Not even a sheep browsed in the lower green, and at the height we had reached there was nothing to browse on.

We did some scrambling along a rock face and gained a shelf that led directly up and onward to the clipper bow. This we eased around, moving almost flat against the rock, and found ourselves at the southern end of a saddle, dotted here and there with sturdy whins and leading for about a mile to another summit. Immediately before us, like a porch, there was a rocky platform where we sat for five minutes, dangling our feet into space. We were quite out of sight of anyone who might be on the western approaches.

"Do you remember Loch Coruisk?" my father asked.

A few years before, we had been to Skye, and I vividly recalled our pony trek from Sligachan to the most baleful of all Highland sea lochs.

"Auber is much the same," said the Boss. "The end of

the world, let in through a crack from the sea. Even on a day like this, it'll be black. And according to local lore, of course, it has no bottom."

It was not a great deal farther, he explained. Once we had crossed the saddle and gained the summit, which was called Ben Weevie, we should have a straight stretch to the brink above Loch Auber.

"And there we'll have some lunch. As for the way back" —I had stuck in a question—"as for the way back, the easiest trail is north—very easy indeed, much less of a climb than this one."

We started off then, slipping and scrambling our way across the saddle, which, while reasonably rounded, was not wide. Halfway over, I had the horrid feeling that someone was watching us, and in turning to look behind, I lost my footing and skidded ten feet down the right-hand slope. The Boss observed my crablike return to the ridge.

"Keep your eyes on the road, boy," he said.

And still there was no sight or sound of pursuit. And the flat clouds threw long shadows, turning green hills to purple.

As I've said, I'm not trying to write a guidebook—and I realize that I've already indulged in considerable scenery. But Loch Auber was everything my father had predicted. On the farther side of Ben Weevie, our going ended abruptly at the brink of a drop clear to sea level, and below us an oval of blue-black ink lay within mighty granite walls. At the far end of it a slot in the cliffs—an opening astonishingly narrow from where we stood—gave access to the sea and the blue sky. But in the tarn itself there was nothing but blackness—dark water with no knowledge of the sun—and all around the cruelty of rocks.

My vocabulary, as usual, was inadequate. "That," I said, "is something!"

But my father was looking off to the eastern side of our pinnacle, where deep valleys, padded with gorse, led down and away from the loch to less shocking and less spectacular country. He was scanning, I realized, the easier route to our eyrie.

Turning abruptly, he said, "Let's have lunch."

We had both cadged sandwiches early in the morning from a "tweeny" in the castle kitchen. (She was down at five, she told us, "to brew cook's tea.") A sample of cook's tea was in my father's flask.

I asked the question that was gnawing at me. "Do you really think he'll come?"

He took a bite of his sandwich. "He may come and he may not. But now that you've seen Loch Auber, I want *you* to go."

"Go? Go where?" I couldn't believe my ears. "Why go?"

"For two reasons," he said. "One—because we've had a good day and I've an appointment." His voice was as casual as a slipper. "And two—because in the event that I am—er —delayed, I think Inspector Black might want to be informed of my last address." He saw my look of protest at the phrase and went on quickly. "These are orders, Jonathan, and you've always been pretty good about orders.

"You will go down the east approach—the left fork, so I can watch you—and you'll keep your eyes wide open for what they may see. About two miles along, the forks come together, and at that point there's a spring and a tumbledown croft—it was once a tripper's *suidhe,* a resting place for hikers, I suppose. Wait there till five o'clock—you have your watch? Good. Keep out of sight; then if I've not joined you, proceed west around the foot of Ben Weevie and hit the shore road back to headquarters. When you get there —if it's under those circumstances—call out the cavalry."

I knew him. I knew him pretty well with his two reasons for my departure. There was a third—I was sure of it—and it lay in his sensing new danger. Thinking the matter over on our way, he had decided I must be out of it. I knew him. He was putting my safety, as he always did, ahead of his own—at the expense of his own, indeed.

But when I tried to protest, he was adamant. "You will do exactly what you're told, no more and no less." His voice was not unkind. "If you stay up here, I'm likely to trip over you."

So I left him on the brink of Loch Auber and made my way down the passage that he had indicated. When I looked back, he had ceased to follow my going and had sat down on a rock, his back to the approaches and his face to the water. The loch was directly beneath him. I remembered his description of it: "The end of the world, let in through a crack from the sea."

I must confess that, being of two minds, I made no remarkable speed. My father's order was one that offended my pride—I had taken pretty good care of myself, surely, during the past few days—and with all my respect for his skill at solo scouting, I felt concerned for him, alone there on the crag so far above Loch Auber. I told myself that if the doctor wanted information from him—and particularly if the Boss were the only one who had it—the probability of violence was small; hand to hand, my father, slight as he was, could outmatch most men. Nor would the mere display of a weapon make him talk. The shooting and the bomb at Inchdarroch had been for psychological effect, I thought—*Schrecklichkeit*. I felt a little more comfortable. Perhaps we were not being trailed at all.

The downward way curved right and left, and what there was of moss-grown turf attained a pleasant springiness. I could no longer see the heights from which I had come, for a secondary shoulder rose between. From time to time I scanned the lonely landscape: as far as I could tell, it was starkly uninhabited.

Two miles down (my father had said) the forks would come together at the site of a spring and a ruined croft. He thought it had been a resting place for hikers. The *suidhe* was to be my post—till five o'clock. My watch read three as I sighted the tumble-down cottage, squat and gray and nearly thatchless. Slithering down a steepish bit of trail I put on brakes and peered ahead with caution. There was no sign of company—but you never can tell. Suddenly aware of tiredness, I sat myself down on a bench, which, by its traces of repair, I took to have been placed there in the interests of the trail. I drew a long breath of relaxed weariness.

Then, from inside the door of the deserted croft, a nastily familiar female voice inquired, "Where, for heaven's sake, is your father?"

Of all recurrent up-croppers, Mary Pigtail takes the biscuit.

"Oh *no!*" I said, without getting up from the bench. "Oh no. Please no."

"Oh yes," she said; "and if you'll walk into my parlor, I'll show you an interesting view."

It was pitch-dark inside the croft, except where a single window facing west framed a rectangle of sky. Miss Hamilton was standing by this aperture, and as my eyes grew used to the murk, I saw that she held a potent-looking pair of binoculars.

"Where's your father, Idiot Boy?" Hers was a mind with but a single thought.

"He's either on his way down or perching on the brink of Loch Auber. May I ask, by the way, what *you're* doing on the bonnie, bonnie slopes of Ben Weevie?"

"I saw you go, and I saw you followed," she said. "So I decided to do a spot of following myself."

"You saw us *followed?*"

"I did. He funked the saddle, and I tracked him around the foot."

"You what? He—*who* funked the saddle?"

"I fancy it's one of your friends from Edinburgh. He kept after you till you turned the scaur. Then he went down and around, with me after him. Here," she said, "take a look."

She handed me the glasses and pointed out and up. I could see nothing but bracken, rock, and deep blue air.

"You're blind. Look—you'll see him on the west fork." It occurred to me that Mary Pigtail was excited.

I looked across the deep V-shaped ravine between the parted trails—and caught my breath. I was excited too.

There he was—the burly figure unmistakable, tweed-garbed and hatted, moving slowly up the western fork, a shotgun tucked beneath his arm. Even at the distance from which I viewed him—a good half a mile, I suppose—there was something furtive in his motion. Or as nearly furtive as you can be with ten thousand acres of unpopulated hills around you.

Mary said, "You've let him gain on me. He'd no such

186

start till you arrived. We'll take the east fork and keep him in sight."

"We'll what?" I asked. "We'll no such thing. I'm under orders to wait here for the Boss—who may well be coming down our way this minute." (I wanted to go as badly as she did.)

"He'll not." Mary was very firm. "Your father's sure to wait for that—for that tublike menace. Or else we'll meet him—your father, that is—on our trail. Come on, hero!" Unexpectedly, she took my hand and started to steer me out of the cottage.

"Hero," I said, "is a girl's name. I tell you—I'm expected to wait here."

She loosed her grip. "Very well," she said. "Then you can just stay." Her voice was absolutely merciless. "I'm going up." For a moment she stared at me in the half light of the doorway. "You fool, don't you realize that your father's a sitting duck?"

She wheeled and started up the east fork with long strides.

Casabianca or no, I asked myself. Must the boy stay on the burning deck? It was a moment of torture. But a worthier man once said, "The woman tempted me." With those pigtails flopping their way up the zigzag passage to danger, I was suddenly incapable of letting them go on alone. Presently I was puffing a few feet behind her. She knew I was there but made no sign to acknowledge my allegiance—except that after a more than usually steep bit, she knelt in the whins and, having had a look herself, handed me the glasses.

This time, I made him out at once, still plodding upward. Apparently he was quite unaware of our presence. Apparently, also, he was well ahead in the race for Weevie's peak.

It is necessary here to insert a little more typography. Of the two trails—and in the States they would never be recognized as such—ours, the eastmost, was lower, with a steep rise toward the end. The doctor's chosen route was higher all along and its ascent more gradual. If my father were still where I had left him, he would be visible first to the enemy and then, as we made it over the higher scarp, to ourselves. It was up to us to move swiftly. As they mounted, however, the trails came slowly nearer to each other, the cleft between them narrowing at the top to a mere fifty yards, so that the higher we went, the more cautious we had to be to keep both cover and silence.

This double necessity was rendered the more difficult because the higher we went, the scarcer the cover became, and the noisier the footing—with less turf and more rock. Once Mary slipped, and two sizable stones went skittering down the slope to our right. We threw ourselves flat, but the doctor never turned, and from then on, we moved with such care that our quarry kept substantially ahead. With satisfaction we reached the dividing outcrop that concealed each trail from the other. We were safe now from observation—until we reached the top—and we made more speed, risking our necks as the going grew precipitous. I must say that I have never seen a better female scrambler than Miss H.

The man whom we were trailing could not see us, and we could not see him—until, with a final heave, we pulled ourselves over the upper rocks on the east top and stood on a scree-covered shelf that held us half above the rim. I shall never forget the tableau—one, for the moment, of utter stillness.

Against the clear blue of the sky, the doctor stood in silhouette, a burly form of menace. He had—with remarkable dexterity, I thought—maneuvered himself to a position barely ninety feet in front of us and a somewhat greater distance behind my father. The Boss still sat, wrapped in a summer idyll, his back toward the enemy, and his feet, presumably, dangling above the chasm.

The doctor, who must have taken his position just before our coming, stood stock still, a somewhat pulpy profile. In a minute, I told myself, he will announce his presence, issue his challenge, demand whatever information he knows or thinks my father has.

But he made no sound. Instead, to my total horror, the shape of his gun, dark and slender, rose from its silhouetted slant to horizontal. Like a statue of doom, he stood at careful aim.

I tried to shout, but I had no voice. My hands dug into the scree of the cliffside—grabbing, gripping like paws in panic. Something stiffened me. My right-hand fingers curled about a stone. It was very nearly round, and it felt like a ball. The sound of half a dozen coaches echoed in my ears—"Don't steer it! Follow through!"

. . . And I can see it now—a small round blot of speed arching against the sky. . . . At the same moment, a shot woke the mountains.

✦ 22 ✦

This tale began, as I remember, with my throwing someone out on the Old Field. It ends with my shy on Ben
Weevie. You may, if you wish, regard the two exercises as
parentheses—with a quantity of words between.

To be brief, my missile hit the doctor on his trigger
hand, bashing his fingers before he could fire and knocking
the gun in an arc around his head. The shot came from my
father. He had been observing all the while the useful reflections in a tin plate packed by Tweeny with our sandwiches. His effort caught the doctor in the shoulder—
"Haven't fired under my arm for years," the Boss apolo-
gized.

With the crack of his shot, Mary and I were over our
parapet—I had grabbed the doctor's gun, the doctor
was reeling about like a drunken man, and my father was
facing him, .32 in hand.

The grimmest part came then. Instead of surrendering,
like a sensible villain, Fisher-Finch-van Hoost suddenly
gave a howl like a wolf. None of us was holding him, and as
he broke into a run, no one fired. He was running toward
the place where we had sat for lunch—the crest that over-
looked Loch Auber. Wordless and witless, we watched as

he flung himself out into the sky. There was no sound thereafter.

Thoughtfully, my father pocketed his pistol.

"Jonathan," he said—and I heard the old, old note of parental reproach—"you are still, I trust, at the spring and the croft?"

There, not long after, were we all.

The rest of the summer was uneventful. The Boss and I did some climbing—including Sgurr-nan-Gillean, which I commend to anybody who is an unintimidated acrophile.

I am back at school now, Alec and Tommy Grant both down the hall. I seem to be certain of a spot on the rugger fifteen. Mr. Krohten—who knows why?—has not appeared among the masters. The Christmas vacation is soon to come.

But wait a minute. MacDuff has just brought me a telegram.

This is what it says:

MEET ME GARE DU NORD PARIS TOMORROW NIGHT RUCTIONS IN RUMANIA BRING DINNER CLOTHES AND ICE-PICK HASTA LUEGO BOSS